LOVE NEVER FAILS

Samantha Arran

ARTHUR H. STOCKWELL LTD
Torrs Park   Ilfracombe   Devon
Established 1898
www.ahstockwell.co.uk

British Library Cataloguing-in-Publication Data.
A catalogue record for this book is available
from the British Library.

ISBN 978-0-7223-3915-2
Printed in Great Britain by
Arthur H. Stockwell Ltd
Torrs Park   Ilfracombe
Devon

On the news in October 2007 two more of our young soldiers had been killed in Afghanistan. As always, I groaned and prayed for the bereaved. Usually, although I do not forget I move on.

I began to think in a new way about possible hurt, lack of forgiveness, bitterness and unfairness in the bereaved. What did God want me to do? Pray harder? Then it clicked: I could write something. So, from my imagination and creativity I began this story.

It is set in Derbyshire, where I live (with changed placenames), and Italy. The main characters are high-ranking police officers and Italians.

This is my first story. It is a human story, and it could be real. I enjoyed writing it very much. All the proceeds are going to widespread charities.

I apologise in advance to the Derbyshire police if I have misused their patrol cars.

Chapter 1

On his way to the police station Inspector Mark Young glanced through the window and saw a newspaper board: 'Commander Amanda Has Been Shot'. He instructed the driver to stop to buy a paper, praying, "Oh, dear God, please not that."

The Commander had been shot in the knee and four of her team had been killed.

Four years previously, Amanda's fiancé, Andrew, and two of his colleagues had been killed in action in Afghanistan. Mark was their colonel. Amanda in her grief and anger accused him of negligence and, unknown to her parents, wouldn't allow him to attend the funeral.

He was devastated. He had been exonerated – there had been no way to stop the unexpected explosion; he would have done anything to prevent it happening. He understood that Amanda had spoken in her grief.

She and Andrew had known each other for twenty years, and Mark knew he had been a wonderful Christian man. Most of the men, in their fears of being attacked and attacking, fantasised about women and boasted about their wives and girlfriends, but Andrew never did.

He said he was engaged to a wonderful Christian lady with glorious red hair and changed the subject when he was questioned. He never divulged that she held a senior position in the Met, but Mark thought she must be someone special. He hadn't a girlfriend.

After Andrew was killed he kept in monthly contact with Amanda's parents, who had the greatest respect for him. Mark also kept in monthly contact with the bereaved of the two soldiers killed with Andrew.

Mark's time was up in Afghanistan after several years and as a new start, with his training and expertise, he joined the police as a senior inspector.

He rang Amanda's parents, Lord Justice Jonathan and Lady Teresa Dansie, and learnt that Amanda was in hospital. The specialist surgeon was operating on her knee.

Her leg was put in a firm brace for at least a month, and she needed 24/7 help to ensure that she didn't slip or fall.

In that month they tried to work out how to repair the kneecap, which was shattered – it had been a vicious bullet. An ordinary knee operation was out of the question.

Sir Philip contacted specialists in America, Russia and Germany, hoping they had new technology to help.

Amanda was, of course, heartbroken over the loss of the members of her team – brilliant young men and women with professional futures in front of them.

She had known them for over a year when she was promoted to commander.

After a few days the Judge informed Mark that Amanda had decided to recuperate at Ashwood, her Aunt Cynthia's home in Derbyshire.

Her ex-nanny (she was now working for Amanda's brother, Joshua, and his wife, Nicola, and had been for twelve years with their four children) asked to be released temporarily to care for Amanda. They of course said she would be comfortable with Joan.

Joan recommended a highly trained physiotherapist to be with Amanda, as through the injury she suffered leg cramps day and night.

Lady Cynthia's home was being updated and decorated ready for when her son, Lord Richard, a highly respected financial wizard here and abroad, returned after his marriage to Sarah in America, a keep-fit instructor and showjumper. Lady Cynthia would move into a smaller home so they could be alone.

She suggested going to stay with her sister-in-law, Contessa Sophie, in Italy so the skeleton staff at Ashwood could give their time to Amanda and her carers.

Mark prayed he would have an opportunity of meeting with Amanda.

She was brought very carefully to Ashwood on a stretcher.

Unknown to Mark, Amanda whilst in hospital had fully realised how unfair she had been to him.

Andrew had told her that Mark lived in the Derbyshire area, so she resolved to find him and ask his forgiveness.

She tried to contact him through various security lines, but to no avail. She didn't know he had left the army.

Mark was eventually contacted through the local police and he was filled with hope.

Amanda wrote a letter inviting him to lunch at Ashwood. He was informed that Amanda needed a Christian bodyguard who would help her with swimming therapy, share her love of music, quizzes, etc. and escort her and Joan out and about – and he must love dogs. Mark was to be promoted to chief superintendent the following week, and he had arranged to have a few days leave to go to a Pavarotti concert in Italy. He asked, if Amanda agreed, to fill the role of her bodyguard, and the news was gratefully received by the authorities and Amanda's parents. He would be able to prepare for his new position and stay in contact with the police station through his PA and laptop.

On the Thursday morning a very nervous Mark went to Ashwood and saw Amanda and Joan sitting at a table outside in the warm sunshine. Amanda's dogs – an Alsatian and a Jack Russell, who were trained to be wary of strangers – came to meet him. They were very friendly. Sparky, the Jack Russell, went potty with him. Amanda saw a tall, attractive, immaculately dressed man, and she picked up that he was nervous. Her stomach flipped and her heart melted.

After the greetings, Amanda asked Mark to sit down; then she burst into tears, sobbing, "I am so sorry for my cruelty to you when Andrew was killed. Will you forgive me?"

Mark answered, "I did at the time. I understood your grief. I am so pleased you have agreed to meet me, and I would love to help you if you so wish."

Amanda replied, "Yes please – don't you agree, Joan?"

Joan said, "You only have to look at the dogs to see what a good man the Inspector is."

(Amanda had no idea he had been in contact with her parents

for the last four years, enquiring how she was.)

Mark said, "We will communicate and help each other."

Amanda had been doing a very hard IQ test. Mark told her, "I do these, but haven't this latest."

He and Amanda looked at the very hard question Amanda had been doing and Mark answered it. Amanda realised how intelligent Mark was.

She rang for Mrs Burton, the housekeeper, and Julian, who waited at table and was a general help to Mrs Burton.

After introductions they sat down with a glass of beer each – Amanda had to drink this to build up her strength.

Mrs Burton told them, "The Inspector's room is ready to move into when convenient."

Amanda and Joan were smiling at him.

"I will arrange to move in today."

Mrs Burton said, "Ask Julian if there is anything you need."

"Thank you – I will."

Amanda told him, "I am longing for my swimming therapy."

"I have an afternoon commitment, but will get back for about 5.30 p.m." He looked at Joan for confirmation and suggested, "Twenty minutes will be enough for the first time. You will need some nourishment, Commander."

She said, "I am beginning to feel hungry. It must be the iron injection I had this morning!" (Joan had told him Amanda wasn't eating.)

Everyone was delighted.

"Are you free for lunch?"

He said, "Yes please."

Mrs Burton asked, "Will our fresh watercress mousse, steaks and salad, and home-grown sweet peaches be all right?"

"It certainly will. Please, what time is lunch?"

They all laughed.

Joan fetched the letter Amanda had written to Mark, and smiling he put it in his pocket.

Amanda suggested wines they could have with lunch and told Mark, "My dada supplies the wines."

Mrs Burton and Julian took Mark to see the pool and his room.

During lunch, Amanda told Mark, "The Women's Institute have

invited me to open the Spring Fair at the local Community Hall on Saturday afternoon, replacing my aunt, Lady Cynthia; I have never done anything like that before."

Mark told her, "Everyone will be very glad to meet you."

"The local dress-shop owner is coming after lunch, bringing some dresses for me to choose from," Amanda told him. "I am not a dress person but my trousers will not go over the brace. Also, the hairdresser is coming tomorrow morning to cut my hair; I will have it cut short for the swimming." Amanda asked Mark, "Will you please make sure the security cameras are switched off when I am in the pool?"

"How will you travel, Commander?"

"The transport for the dogs is being installed with more seats and a lift for my chair."

"When will this be completed?"

"I will find out today, Inspector."

Whilst they were having lunch, Mark told them, "I am being promoted next Thursday to chief superintendent."

Amanda and Joan were delighted and they congratulated him.

Amanda asked, "Are you going to celebrate this?"

He replied, "I was going to go on holiday, come back for Thursday and then go back for a few more days."

Amanda asked, "Have you sacrificed this holiday for me?"

"Yes," he replied, "I wanted to meet you and help."

Amanda then asked him, "Would you like to invite your colleagues and friends here for lunch?"

"Yes please. That would be wonderful." (Amanda knew from his details he wasn't married and didn't have a lady friend.)

Amanda then asked, "What about a musical programme in the afternoon?"

"Brilliant! Most of my friends are musical."

Amanda rang Mrs Burton and she was very pleased. Amanda then asked, "Will the chefs from the Morley be able to come?"

Mrs Burton said, "Leave this with me. I will let you have the menus for your approval."

"Right," Amanda said to Mark, "please make a list and invite them. We will fax the menus. Have you any family, Inspector?"

"I live with my father, Inspector Stan, and my brother, Luke, who is a fitness trainer in the local police stations. My younger brother, Adam, is at Cambridge University."

Amanda asked, "Your mother?"

Mark answered, "She left us four months ago. She is living in Spain with a man she met."

Amanda and Joan said how sorry they were.

"Would your father like to come to lunch tomorrow?"

Mark said, "I am positive he will. Thank you, ma'am."

Mark's PA texted him and took him to Brookwell Station, where he confirmed he would be helping the Commander.

Chief Inspector Hawkins asked, "How is she?"

Mark told him, "She would like to meet you; are you free for lunch tomorrow?"

"I'll make sure I am."

"Also, the Commander is hosting a lunch next Thursday after my promotion: will you be able to come to that? It will be followed by a musical programme."

He laughed. "I certainly will. I have arranged a day's leave. We were organising taking you out for lunch, but this will be much better."

Mark showed him the list of the senior police he thought should also be invited and asked Chief Inspector Hawkins to let him know if he thought of anyone else. "This will be a wonderful opportunity to meet the Commander," he said.

Chief Inspector Hawkins jovially told Mark, "You must have made a good impression."

"She is a beautiful, super-intelligent lady and wants to meet the local police."

Mark cleared leave with his superior for the last two weeks Amanda would be there. He then went with his PA into the local town and at a well-known store bought swimming shorts, robe, and underwear. His PA went to get him wet-shaving equipment, toothbrush and toothpaste, so he could freshen up before dinner.

One of the shop assistants alerted the manager, who came rushing to Mark to congratulate him on his promotion – it had

10

been television and newspaper news. Also, the lunchtime news had announced that Mark would be the Commander's helper whilst she was recuperating.

"We have a new line of shorts in, sir." An assistant brought several.

Mark quickly chose three.

The manager asked Mark, "Will you take the Commander, as a welcome to this community, these beauty treatments?"

Mark rang Joan to ask if this was acceptable. Joan said it was and asked him to thank the manager on Amanda's behalf.

On the way back, Mark rang the local menswear shop near the police station and asked for three pairs of summer trousers with socks to match – he hadn't much time left. The Italian outfitter had these ready when Mark arrived and also three summer shirts. Mark then rushed back to get ready for the swim.

He was waiting at the pool when Amanda came in her wheelchair. He and Joan helped her out and into the pool. She was trembling as Mark went first, holding out his hand. All went well, and when she was in the water she said, "This is wonderful! I feel free for the first time since having the brace on."

Joan was crying. She left them and waited outside with her knitting.

After swimming a few strokes, Amanda had cramp in her damaged leg – she suffered with this also during the night.

Joan had warned Mark about the cramp, and he had promised to send the dogs for her if there was a problem; but instead he guided her and while she gripped the side he massaged the leg, releasing the cramp. They stayed there.

Mark said, "I will do anything to help you. I want you to trust me and talk to me about anything."

Amanda put her hand on Mark's shoulder and burst out crying.

The dogs were unsettled and whimpering, so Joan ran in, but when she saw the scene she left them again.

Amanda asked, "How can I forget the members of my team being killed?"

Mark replied, "We will never forget, however well trained we are, but we must keep asking God to help us and to comfort the families. It takes time, Commander."

Amanda said, "Mark" – she used his name for the first time – "I am so sorry I was so cruel to you. I am supposed to be a Christian."

Mark hushed her: "I believe in God and He understands. We are human; we have emotions. If we hadn't, we would be zombies. This is a new beginning for both of us. I love to sing, Commander; I play the organ – I am an organist in our church – I love quizzes and the countryside; I like to watch detectives on the TV and DVDs; my brother Luke and I play computer tennis. That will be good exercise we can do together."

She told him, "Call me Amanda when we are alone or with Joan. We will have to work a programme out. After dinner, Miss Biggin, a fully trained physiotherapist, comes for the night shift; Joan is on call if needed. I then go to my room, ring my dada and mum, my brother Joshua and his wife, Nicola, the Contessa, and others or fax; I do a simple workout with Miss Biggin, then prepare for bed; I write my diary then I usually watch a detective series or read."

Mark said, "If it will help you and the Contessa, I could set up a computer camera link so you can see each other as you converse. You will have to sit in front of the screen."

Amanda said, "I would love that. I will tell my aunt this evening."

Mark promised: "I will get it set up at both ends." (He spoke fluent Italian.)

Chapter 2

Amanda, Joan and Mark met up for dinner. Mark had already received some replies for the promotion lunch – everyone wanted to be remembered to Amanda and they were all greatly looking forward to meeting her.

After dinner Miss Biggin came. She was very pleased to meet Mark.

He went home to fetch his computer equipment, his keyboard, etc. His dad was thrilled to be invited to lunch the next day.

Luke asked, "When am I going to meet the Commander?"

Mark said, "She is hosting a lunch for me next Thursday and you are both, of course, invited. Then we are going to have a musical afternoon."

They said, "Wow!"

"Also, the Commander is opening the Ashwood Spring Fair on Saturday."

When he returned to Ashwood, with Amanda's permission he whistled for her dogs and took them for a walk down to the river; he was feeling very happy and thanking God.

On Friday morning the hairdresser and his assistants arrived. Whilst Amanda was having a manicure and the beautician was finding suitable make-up for her, Clove went to cut Mark's hair. Amanda had invited Sandra, who waited at table and cleaned her rooms, to come and attend to her hair and face; Sandra was excited at this honour and welcomed the extra money.

Clove was thrilled with Amanda's hair, which curled and waved naturally. After cutting and conditioning, he gave Amanda a new style, and it really suited her. He said, "You need a good conditioner if you swim often."

Amanda showed him the presents she had received.

He told her, "These are excellent!"

Then the beautician gave Amanda a delicate makeover.

They all looked forward to coming back the next day to prepare her for the Spring Fair. Joan sent Lady Teresa a photograph of Amanda with her new hairstyle. She was thrilled. Amanda had previously never taken much interest in her appearance, apart from looking immaculate and always wearing well-fitted clothes.

Amanda and Joan went down to meet Chief Inspector Hawkins and Mark's father. Amanda thought Chief Inspector Hawkins was going to kiss her! They were so pleased to meet her and said how beautiful she was. Amanda laughed and blushed. Mark laughed too.

Amanda asked, "Would you like a drink?"

They all had a glass of beer each.

Chief Inspector Hawkins had brought Amanda a CD of the local male-voice choir. She said, "I will listen to this as soon as possible."

They went in to lunch. Chief Inspector Hawkins asked about her programme.

She said, "Inspector Mark and I are going to swim morning and teatime – this is the best exercise for my leg."

Joan said, "Yes, but next week you will not be able to swim for a few days."

Amanda blushed and didn't know where to look.

Joan said, "They had to know for your programme."

Amanda looked at Mark. He laughed and they all joined in.

Amanda told them, "Joan was my nanny."

They asked Joan, "What kind of child was she?"

"A beautiful girl – always running in the wood behind her home, playing and caring for animals. Her brother Joshua is three years older and they were the best of friends, but Amanda at only three years threw his friends about. Some of them rang first; and if she was at home, they didn't come."

They all laughed and Amanda said, "I wasn't having them thinking they could bully Joshua."

Joan laughed: "Joshua could well look after himself. It was

just an excuse – you liked throwing them about."

Amanda said, "I was a pain."

They discussed who was coming to Mark's promotion lunch, and whether there were any they had missed. Chief Inspector Hawkins suggested two more and Mark said he would invite them after lunch. Inspector Stan suggested Matthew, the vicar of The Open Church, where they worshipped.

Mark told them, "Earlier this morning, the vicar from the local St James' Church asked Matthew if they could borrow an organist for this Sunday as their regular organist is away. Matthew suggested me because I know the music; but if I can't manage it, he will arrange someone else."

Amanda said, "I would love to go to worship God to thank Him for sending me to this area, and to hear you playing."

Inspector Stan said he also would.

"We will arrange transport when we know how many are going," Amanda told them.

Amanda asked Chief Inspector Hawkins, "Would you like to go with us and come here for lunch?"

He thanked her. "It is my sister's birthday and her husband has booked us a table, but I would like to go to St James' with you."

Amanda told them, "The men are catching the first trout early Sunday morning."

Chief Inspector Hawkins said, "Ooo! I love trout – may I come for breakfast?"

They all laughed and Amanda said, "Of course, I have been missing my dada so much, but with you and Inspector Stan I am not feeling so homesick now. May I think of you two as my favourite adopted uncles?"

They were very pleased at this and said, "We will help you with anything – you only have to ask."

Amanda thanked them.

Chief Inspector Hawkins (Bob) asked, "What is your programme after your knee has been attended to, ma'am?"

Amanda said, "I am going back midweek to the Met, doing desk work. I will stay with my adored parents and animals and intend coming back to Ashwood for weekends until my cousin,

Lord Richard, returns after marrying Sarah, an American lady. Lady Cynthia is moving into a smaller home, but by then I will be working full-time."

Bob told her, "Everyone is pleased you are opening the Spring Fair. They all want to meet you."

Amanda admitted, "I am very nervous; I haven't done anything like this before."

They all assured her: "You will be brilliant."

Amanda asked them to help her to think of something to say which related to people in the area.

Stan suggested, "You men, open your wallets and let the moths fly out."

They all laughed again and Amanda said, "Thank you. I will use that." She then said, "I feel guilty about laughing when members of my team have been killed."

Bob advised, "You have to put that behind you – this is the world we are living in, and we have to enjoy each new day as it comes."

Amanda told them, "Inspector Mark is helping me greatly."

Stan said, "I was going to my sisters in Bruxton for a few days before Mark's promotion, but I have delayed this until after tomorrow so I can attend the Spring Fair."

Amanda gently said, "Inspector Mark has told me and Joan of his mother going off to Spain."

"Yes," said Stan, "we thought there was something, because she started dressing younger and going out on her own. I know there have been many times when I have neglected her through pressure of work, but I am easing down now for retirement and I have planned holidays and activities we can do together. Luke, whom Mark has told you about, is going to Germany on Monday until Wednesday for the football matches, so our housekeeper is going on holiday with her husband for a few days."

Amanda asked, "Will you be on your own?"

"No, I have my dog and Mark's – and there is plenty of food in the freezer."

Amanda looked at Mark then asked his dad, "If it is OK with Mrs Burton, would you like to come here and bring both dogs – I adore dogs."

She rang Mrs Burton, who immediately said, "There is an

en-suite room near Inspector Mark's. I know the Inspector's situation and he will be very welcome here."

Amanda passed that message on to him. "Please bring the dogs – what breeds are they?"

"Mark's is a Labrador he found abandoned and hurt; mine's a golden retriever."

Mark was overwhelmed and thankful that his dad and their dogs were able to come.

Amanda said, "That's all right, then." (This was one of her sayings.)

Stan suggested, "I could in move tomorrow."

"Fine," said Amanda, "I will let Mrs Burton and Julian know. Julian will take care of you both." (Amanda was paying him and Sandra extra money from an insurance scheme she was in.)

"I will pay."

Amanda smiled. "You are covered by my insurance as you will be part of security!"

They all laughed at this and Amanda went on: "This is a holiday for you, Inspector Stan."

She then asked, "Where locally can I buy music and words for 'You'll Never Walk Alone'?

They told her the name of a local shop, and Mark rang them. Graham Mitchell, the owner, promised to have it ready for the next day.

Chief Inspector Hawkins said, "A patrolling police car will pick it up."

Graham then said, "I will be at the Spring Fair. Will you please convey to the Commander how thrilled everyone in the area is at her choosing Ashwood to recuperate in?"

Mark thanked him and, in the background, Amanda thanked him.

Joan told Inspector Stan, "Whilst the Commander is working through her routine after dinner, I play bridge with Mrs Burton and a few friends. We also do different activities here in the evenings. You will be most welcome when you are free."

With tears in his eyes he said, "Thank you very much. In the daytime for the next few days I will be able to take all the dogs walking."

Chief Inspector Hawkins asked, "Am I included in these evenings?"

Joan said, "I am sure you will be most welcome, and afterwards I hope you will stay for a light supper and hot drink."

Amanda asked, "Are you married?"

He replied, "I am a widower. Early in our marriage my wife had a miscarriage and they found she had a heart murmur so couldn't have children. She died from a heart attack five years ago." Amanda and Joan expressed their sorrow, and he said, "We had had a wonderful thirty-one years. She was my best friend – I could talk to her about anything. You will appreciate that in my work I have to be dedicated and, like Stan, I wasn't always at home. But she understood my commitment and supported me. I greatly miss her." He added, "My sister and her husband came to live with me and I have domestic help."

Amanda suggested, looking at Mark, "Would you like to have a sing-song this afternoon before the swimming therapy?"

They all said, "Love to!"

Amanda asked Stan, "Have you any hobbies?"

He said, "Sketching and painting, which I haven't done for years. I love walking with the dogs, playing golf, bridge, etc. I hope to buy an old car to renovate when I retire next month. I considered staying on, but Mark said I had done enough. He wants me to enjoy my leisure."

She asked, "Have you a car in mind?"

He answered, "No, not yet."

Amanda looked at Mark and Joan and said, "I may be able to help you – may I make a call?"

She rang Andrew's parents, and Andrew's dad, Ian, answered. He was amazed: "Darling Amanda, we were going to ring you this afternoon!" (They kept in close contact.) "Georgina is out just now. How are you today?"

She said, "Much stronger." In her forthright manner she asked, "Ian darling, have you still got Andrew's cars and bits?"

He answered, "Yes, do you want them?"

"I know someone who does, and who will take great care of them."

Excitement rippled round the table.

"Amanda sweetheart, I may as well tell you now but Georgina will ring you later – we are selling up and moving to Portugal. You know how we love it, and lots of our friends have retired and settled there. We didn't want to say anything until it was finally settled and until you were stronger. We were wondering what to do with the cars, so please accept them. You will be doing us such a big favour. We didn't want just anyone to have them. Let us know the destination and we will transport them – it will be our pleasure. It will make Georgina so happy to know they are going to a good home. And, Amanda darling, Portugal is only two hours away. We want you to be happy. You are a beautiful young woman and it is time you came out of your mourning for Andrew. It is what he would want. He knew the dangers he was going into. You and we are very proud of him."

"I am, Ian – very proud. He will always live on in my heart."

"We will ring you later, darling. What time will be convenient?"

"With my new exercise programme, is 9 p.m. OK?"

"Fine. Speak to you then. Love you."

"Love you too, darling Ian."

She put the phone down and they waited for her to speak. She was holding Mark's hand. She then said, "That was really God's timing." She told them about Portugal.

Bob said, "My faith in God has never been strong but this is making me think."

Amanda then told Stan, "There are six cars, but perhaps Joan would like one of them. We need to sort out where they are to be delivered to."

They then took time to give thanks to God for His timing and prayed for the success of Ian and Georgina's move to Portugal.

"Commander, if I have a car ready, may I enter it for the Chatsworth House Country Fair parade in September, in honour of Andrew?"

With tears in her eyes, she said, "Thank you, Inspector. I would love that. I will let Andrew's parents know. They will be so grateful."

Amanda told them, "I was so disappointed that I couldn't travel to Italy to be with my beloved aunt, Contessa Sophie; she has a heart condition now which prevents her from travelling."

Chief Inspector Hawkins asked, "Has she a husband and family?"

"No. It was tragic: her husband of two weeks, Count Vincentia Gambetti's hobby was motorcycle racing. Aunt Sophie knew this when she fell in love with him. She admired his dare-devil ways but always urged him to be careful. He promised he would. He had everything to live for with her and the family they would have. He was riding his powerful motorcycle in pouring rain when he skidded on a patch of oil, crashed and died instantly. Aunt Sophie has never recovered, but she made a career running his property businesses. She invested in many businesses, greatly helping the economy in Italy, London and Bryden. She is very highly respected. We have shared a great bond since I was very young. I spend as much time as possible with her. She loves music as I do, and Pavarotti is a personal friend of hers. She is beautiful, isn't she, Joan?"

Joan replied, "She is a beautiful lady and Amanda has made her life worth living."

Amanda added, "She would not give up her cigarettes, though. Count Luca, who often flies us to Italy, is a personal friend; he spends a lot of time with Aunt. He has been married three times and has two sons: Lorenzo is married with a son and daughter, Santorini is still single." (Luca had hoped Amanda would marry one of his sons, but they thought she was a cold fish as she had no interest in nightclubs and casual sex. However, they were good friends.) "The three of them are billionaires through their aeroplane and shipping businesses. The Contessa has shares in these businesses. She helped Luca set up the aeroplane business and he has flourished since then."

Amanda and Joan went upstairs to freshen up and then they all went into the music room and requested Amanda play for them. She played two light-classical pieces. They were enthralled. Then they had a sing-song together. Amanda asked Mark to play his organ keyboard. She was thrilled listening to him. Then they all sang again.

After afternoon tea, Bob reluctantly went back to the station, Stan went home to organise moving in, and Amanda and Mark prepared for their swim.

Chapter 3

On Saturday, Amanda was in one of her new dresses ready for the Spring Fair. Joan sent photographs taken on her mobile phone to Lady Teresa and Amanda's sister-in-law, Nicola, who was co-editor of a fashion magazine. They were delighted at Amanda's new look and relieved that she was coming out of her depression.

Amanda and Joan went down to meet Luke, Mark's brother, who told Amanda, "After my short holiday, as you get stronger I will help work out suitable exercise therapy for you."

She said, "I am delighted to tell you that I have woken up from cramp only twice recently."

Miss Biggin, Amanda's physiotherapist, joined them for lunch before going with them to the Spring Fair.

During lunch, Luke asked Amanda about her fitness programme in London. When she told him he was greatly impressed and said, "Not many of my men could achieve that level."

Mark said, "The Commander is SAS-trained."

"Wow!"

Amanda told Luke, "I need a workout to keep my arms and body firm and supple. Perhaps there is a machine I could hire?"

Luke promised her he would look into it.

When they arrived at Ashwood Community Hall, Amanda was in her chair so she could get around better without any danger of falling. Mrs Burton and Joan went to help in the kitchen; Luke and the inspectors helped to put more tables and chairs outside; whilst Amanda, Mark and Miss Biggin went to meet the stallholders.

Amanda and Miss Biggin bought several items, and, when they

came to the dressmaker's stall and met Jean again (who had altered her dress for that day), Amanda bought nightdresses and other items. Jean showed her a dress she had made. It was in Amanda's colours and size, and it was a dress suitable for wearing to church. Amanda was eager to buy it, and Jean said, "Of course, if it doesn't fit, I will alter it on Monday afternoon when I come to Ashwood." Amanda also asked Jean to make her some culottes so she wouldn't be embarrassed swinging her leg getting in and out of the car, etc.

The chairperson introduced Amanda as 'Commander and Lady Amanda' and thanked her for stepping in for Lady Cynthia. She thanked her and Lady Cynthia for their donations.

Amanda opened with, "I am very pleased to be in this community! As you know, I have been before but only briefly to the horse trials as I spend as much time as possible with my beloved aunt, the Contessa, in Italy." She went on, "This is a first for me," and then she invited people to enjoy themselves and give to the good cause. She invited the men to open their wallets "and let the moths fly out!"

Everyone clapped, cheered and whistled. Many of the crowd, including the local newspaper reporters, took photographs. Then the chairperson gave Amanda a framed enlarged photograph of her on her horse, Tarquin, jumping at Ashwood.

Amanda said, "I am thrilled. I will keep it for ever. At the moment I couldn't do this jump."

Everybody clapped.

She ended by telling them about the videos she had made to greet her horse, Tarquin, and her Rottweiler, Thunder, morning and evening so they wouldn't miss her. She added, "They must be fed up with these and they are probably thinking 'Don't they realise we have brains?'"

Everybody laughed.

A man called out, "Excuse me, ma'am, did you win *Celebrity Charity Quiz?*"

She laughed. "You will have to watch it next Saturday evening."

Mark fetched the photograph. There were several whistles, Amanda and Mark laughed, and then Joan took her to a table set up for them under a large umbrella.

The local newspaper and magazine reporters asked if they could take more photographs, and if she would say a few words.

She said, "I am very pleased to be in this community, and I hope to meet more people as I get stronger." She then thanked everyone for their flowers and welcome gifts.

Later, as they were drinking cups of tea, people came up to say hello and that they were pleased to meet her. Geoff, one of the dog-trainers, came and apologised to Amanda for interrupting but he said he had an urgent message: 'Hercules and Thor are needed and the Met are sending a helicopter.' Amanda asked, "Do you know how long they will be away?"

"At least two or three days, ma'am – maybe longer. Sir," he asked Mark, "may I have a word?"

Outside on their own, Geoff said, "London has had a massive breakthrough. The man who shot the Commander is so repentant that he has given the Met valuable information about terrorists; also there is such great fear that other informants have come forward. Special Branch and the SAS are moving in this afternoon. Everyone is so proud of the Commander. It is unlikely that this can be traced back to the Commander, but she will be shadowed for the time being."

Geoff rushed off.

Amanda suggested to Mark, "We will have to make sure Cambridge and Oxford aren't lonely. This is a good opportunity to get them used to being separated and being with the other dogs. I would also like the dogs to come muzzled with the others to the pool."

Her companions asked her, "What is happening now to Cambridge and Oxford?" They knew they were not now 100% and couldn't be Met sniffer dogs.

Amanda said, "I have bought them. When they are fit enough they will be put to stud and their puppies will be trained."

Amanda signalled to Joan and Miss Biggin that she needed to go to the loo. They had brought a new equipment because the Community Hall hadn't a disabled toilet. There was much laughter as this equipment was used with Mark guarding the door. He was laughing when they came out.

Amanda asked, "Have you been listening?"

"No."

She said, laughing, "Fibber!"

They went back to their table and a couple who had been waiting came up with a gorgeous Italian man called Cristiano.

Mr and Mrs Goodall owned the Bryden glassware factory, which supplied Mason's store in London, owned by her mum, brother Joshua and the Contessa.

Amanda said, "I am so pleased to meet you and I will tell my family. Have you plenty of orders?"

Mr Goodall said, "With grateful thanks to your family, ma'am." (They had been on the point of making the workforce redundant when they received their first order from the London store; this was a new beginning for the community and gave a boost to local commerce.)

They introduced Cristiano, who told Amanda, "My parents have bought Pascali, the Italian store near the Contessa." (They had three other stores. He was a director, and the Contessa had shares in these stores.) "I am over here, ma'am, at the Contessa's recommendation, to buy glassware from Mr and Mrs Goodall for our stores. This is a new line we are introducing." Cristiano then asked in Italian, "Will you have dinner with me this evening at the Morley, or wherever you choose? I am returning to Italy tomorrow to set up the contract."

Amanda charmingly thanked him, saying, "I have a previous engagement. It is arranged, but next time I am with my aunt I hope you, as a friend, and your parents will come for a meal."

He looked disappointed but laughingly said, "You cannot blame a man for trying."

Mark said in Italian, "Of course not."

Smiling, Cristiano bowed. He gave Amanda a case which contained shampoos, conditioners, several beauty treatments and make-up: "Please accept this. It is one of our new lines. Will you let the Contessa know your opinion of these products?"

"With pleasure!" She was delighted.

Cristiano said, kissing her hand, "I hope to see you next time you come to Italy. We now have to go to the factory."

Mrs Goodall gave Amanda a box which contained twelve wine glasses decorated with sweet peas, leaves and a small cross. She adored them.

"You must have known that I love sweet peas."

Mark introduced two more couples (senior police and their wives). Amanda apologised for not inviting the wives to the lunch: "You will appreciate the lunch is for Mark and his colleagues."

They said, "Of course," and they asked about the musical programme.

She replied, "Inspector Mark and I are setting this up. I am greatly looking forward to this."

Chief Constable Blake said, "We all are, and we are pleased to have this opportunity of meeting you."

Mrs Blake said, "You are so beautiful, Commander, and so slim – you have put me to shame. I will have to do something about this."

Mrs Ward agreed. "Same here!"

They all laughed.

Amanda showed them the wine glasses Mr and Mrs Goodall had just given her.

They said, "We could do with new glassware. We will go to the Bryden shop." She also showed them the shampoos, etc. that Cristiano had given her and she explained that it was a new line he was selling in his Italian stores.

Mrs Blake said, "You don't need beauty treatments, Commander."

Amanda replied, "I will need moisturisers after so much swimming."

Chief Constable Blake then asked, "How are you getting on with Mark, ma'am?"

She replied, "We have a great affinity. I have been much more settled since he, Chief Inspector Hawkins and Inspector Young have come. The transition from being super-active to virtually not being able to move without help has been hard for me."

They sympathised.

Chief Inspector Ward then said, "Mark has pulled out all the stops to be your helper. Did you know he has given up his holiday in Italy and going to the Pavarotti concerts, Commander?"

"No," she said, "I didn't know that."

Mark said, "I can go to Italy another time. I wanted to help you."

Amanda told them, "The Contessa is sending me CDs of the concerts. I will get copies for Inspector Mark, and we will be able to listen to them together."

Mark put Bob in the picture about the arrests and said that Amanda would be shadowed for the time being. The Chief Inspector assured Mark that no one would hurt Amanda. Bob then said, "What a wonderful lady!" and Mark agreed. They were pleased that she had chosen their area in which to recuperate.

Chief Inspector Ward said, "If there is anything we can do to help you, ma'am, let us know through Mark. You are in good hands."

Amanda agreed.

At 4.30 Joan said, "It is time to go."

They said goodbye and everyone thanked them for coming.

Bob, Luke and a few of his colleagues stayed and helped put the tables and chairs away. The WI had never had such a good response and the money taken was outstanding.

On the way back they all told Amanda, "You have done a good job. We are very proud of you; you have been so natural and relaxed. Everyone is uplifted by the afternoon."

Luke sent Amanda's parents, Joshua and Nicola a film of the afternoon which had been taken on his mobile phone; they also were all very proud of her and told her so when she rang them after dinner.

Bob told Mark on the quiet that he would send a dog handler with two guard dogs to cover the nights Geoff and the dogs were away. He had promised Amanda's father he would make sure she had protection along with Mark. Amanda and Mark had their swim, and Cambridge and Oxford settled down with the other dogs and came outside Amanda's room whilst she showered and changed. They stayed with her through the night without the muzzles. She was very pleased and proud of them.

Chapter 4

On Sunday, breakfast was at 7 a.m. Mark and Luke had to get to St James' Church for the 9.30 one-hour service as Mark was playing the organ. He hadn't been there before. Mark was one of the regular organists at The Open Church.

Bob came for breakfast. The men had caught plenty of trout, and they all tucked in! It was cooked to perfection, as was everything else. Amanda and the others left in good time for the 11 a.m. service, which was informal and geared for families. Everyone was looking forward to them coming.

When they arrived, Mark was playing the organ, practising with the choir for the next service. Amanda tried to listen to him but had to be polite to everyone. Afterwards she remarked to the Reverend Brian how his message had related to a situation in the world at this time. He was very pleased and encouraged.

Amanda asked, "Is your family here?"

He said, "No, my daughter, Liz, is at Cambridge University. It is her birthday and my wife has gone down to see her. Liz is revising for exams."

Amanda asked, "Are you on your own?"

He said, "My son Robert is with me."

"Would you like to come to Ashwood for lunch?"

He accepted with delight.

The handlers had dropped Amanda and Bob at the church and came back to pick them up.

Brian said, "I will come in my car."

Luke said, "We have space. If you're not driving, you can have a glass or two of wine!"

Mark brought Reverend Hugh, his wife, Rachel, and son,

Richard, to be introduced. He had met Hugh in the course of his police work.

Amanda asked Mrs Burton if they could also come. She said, "There will be plenty."

The family accepted with joy.

Lady Cynthia's chef was on holiday so two lady cooks from the village had stepped in to help Amanda.

Bob rang the local police station and asked if they had a patrol car to take friends back to Ashwood. They promised one would be with them in a few minutes!

Over a delicious lunch, Brian remarked on the quality of the wines.

Amanda told them, "My dada sent them. They were produced from grapes not mixed." She said, "My dada teaches me about wines."

Amanda then had an attack of cramp. Mark and Joan quickly massaged it away, explaining it was the damage to her knee which caused this. She didn't get it as many times as she had, but it still woke her during the night sometimes.

They said, "We will pray about this."

She replied, "Please do."

Reverend Brian said, "What a worthwhile job police work is!"

Amanda replied, "Yes, but yours is more precious. We arrest the criminals and try to keep law and order, but your ministry leads people to know Jesus, whereby they learn it is wrong to murder, steal, abuse, etc."

Brian and Hugh were very encouraged by these words.

They were all very comfortable with one another. The conversation flowed.

Mark said, "Commander, Reverend Brian has lent me the music and words we need for Thursday afternoon and a memory stick with other words. Luke will transfer these onto the screen." He went on, "Reverend Brian and Reverend Hugh are good singers and very musical."

She said, "We could do with you for Thursday. We are having a lunch and musical programme to celebrate Inspector Mark's promotion." Amanda asked Brian and Hugh, "Are you free?"

"We will make sure we are!"

Mark promised them, "You will be picked up at 12 p.m."

28

Amanda then said, "It is a male time, apart from Joan and myself. I couldn't invite the wives. It is for Inspector Mark's colleagues, and Joan and I are looking forward to meeting them. Please let Mark know what you will be singing and we will put this into the programme; also we will let you have the menus before you go home."

Reverend Hugh asked, "Are you singing, ma'am?"

"Yes, I love to sing, and to play the piano and guitar. Inspector Mark is also singing and his colleagues are taking part. We will end with a rousing community sing-song."

Brian and Hugh both said, "It sounds marvellous. Thank you for inviting us."

Amanda and Joan went upstairs, and the staff showed the guests to the rest room. They later met up outside for coffee under the big canopy, and then, with Amanda in her chair, they walked the dogs down to the river.

Hugh asked, "Are you coming to evensong?"

Joan said, "No, Lady Amanda has travelled enough for today. She is going for her swimming therapy with Inspector Mark."

Inspector Stan and Luke took the dogs for a walk.

Amanda told them, "My night nurse, Miss Biggin, is a fully trained physiotherapist. On Sundays we eat at 7.30 so she comes a little earlier to share this meal with us. Afterwards I ring my dada and mum, my brother, Joshua, and his wife, Nicola, and then my aunt, the Contessa, in Italy. Inspector Mark is setting up a computer camera link with the Contessa so we can speak face-to-face. My aunt cannot travel now – she has a weak heart – so it will be very precious for me to see her face."

Mark told her, "My contact in Italy should have completed setting it up by this evening."

Amanda was so glad.

Brian asked Mark, "Do you speak Italian?"

He said, "Yes."

Amanda said, "Fluently – we converse in Italian."

They asked, "Is it time for us to leave?"

Mark said, "We have the swimming therapy at 5.30; the Commander gets cramp, so she can only manage twenty minutes just now. We swim morning and teatime."

29

Amanda told them, "It is my best exercise just now; I do a gentle workout in my room with Miss Biggin before I prepare for bed."

After their walk they went back to the outside table for a cup of tea.

Mark told them, "My younger brother is at Cambridge taking a management degree. Adam is a wonderful illustrator. He could easily earn his living doing this, but he is hoping to get a job with the police. He is coming next weekend – he is too busy studying like all the others at the moment."

Amanda asked Robert, "Are you studying or working?"

He replied, "I am unemployed, Commander. I keep applying for jobs but so far have been unsuccessful."

Brian said, "Robert is a computer whizz."

Amanda said, "I could do with some help to send out thank-you letters to all who have sent flowers and gifts." Amanda looked at Mark, and he nodded. "Are you willing to help us sort out the cards for replies? We need to find their addresses."

Robert said, "I would love to. I have a programme where I can print out your handwriting, ma'am."

She asked, "Is tomorrow morning convenient? I will be thankful when these have been sent."

"Yes, ma'am, I will be here early."

"How will you get here?"

"My dad will lend me his car" – grinning at his dad.

Amanda went on: "We will need the white card for the place cards on Thursday."

Stan said, "I will fetch some tomorrow morning from Chesterton."

Robert offered to call on his way.

Stan said, "It is market day. The town will be packed, but I can park at the station."

Reverend Brian said, "I can send the paper and envelopes – best quality – and white card from the church office. Please accept these as a gift."

"Thank you," said Amanda, "but send me an invoice so I can ask you again."

Robert said he would call at the village post office for the stamps, and Mrs Burton brought the money from petty cash. Mark then asked Amanda if he could ring Adam to design the letterhead and place cards.

"Yes please, if he is not too busy."

Brian had to leave for the evensong, but Robert suggested, "I could stay a while if now is convenient to make a start."

Amanda welcomed this.

Hugh and family offered, "We could stay also, if it is OK."

"It certainly is, thank you."

Amanda rang Mrs Burton to ask if the guests could stay for dinner as they were helping her with the thank-you letters.

She said, "Of course, ma'am," and they accepted the invitation with joy.

Joan fetched a large box with the cards in and then took Amanda upstairs; Luke collected the telephone directories, for Robert and them to start finding the addresses. Mark rang Adam, who said he would with pleasure let them have designs for early tomorrow morning.

Amanda had discomfort in her stomach. She quietly asked Joan to take her upstairs.

Joan looked at Mark and told him, "The Commander will not be swimming today. We will join you shortly."

Robert – bless him! – assured Amanda, "My mum and sister have this monthly problem."

They all burst out laughing and Richard grinned.

"I understand, ma'am," he said. "I have learnt all about this at school."

Amanda thanked them and said, "I am so relaxed with all of you. I hope we are able to meet often whilst I am here. I am getting stronger each day." She glanced at Mark. He looked crestfallen, so she smiled up at him. "Of course, I will be spending the majority of my time with Inspector Mark and working out our routine."

He smiled back at her, and she understood. A wave of happiness went through both of them. He accompanied them upstairs. Mrs Burton and Julian came to attend to the guests.

Joan explained to him, "I expected Amanda's having some discomfort as her daily activities are curtailed just now."

He looked upset. "Have I to ask the guests to leave?" he asked.

Amanda quickly reassured him: "I will be OK after I have had a couple of painkillers. I will be so thankful to get the acknowledgements out. Then we will be able to really concentrate on your Thursday lunch and the afternoon."

"Thank you. I will fetch my laptop to help Robert."

"We will be down shortly," Joan smilingly told him.

They were all still sorting out the addresses. Luke said, "It is quite an undertaking but between us we are off to a good start." He asked, "Have we a guillotine to cut the name cards?"

Robert said, "I will bring one tomorrow."

Miss Biggin joined them.

Amanda told them, "It is a shame I received so many flowers. I really didn't know what to do with them all, so I sent some to the local hospitals and hospices."

They enjoyed the meal, and then Luke took their new friends and dropped them off on his way home.

Mark, Miss Biggin and Amanda sat outside for a while. It was still warm after a beautiful day. Joan and Inspector Stan took the dogs down to the river.

Amanda reflected, "What a gorgeous day it has been, meeting our new friends and how relieved I am for the acknowledgments going out! I can't wait to see Adam's designs."

Next morning Adam sent beautiful illustrations to Mark's computer. Mark texted his and Amanda's thanks and said he looked forward to seeing him at the weekend.

Robert arrived with all the equipment and put in the heading which Adam had sent. Printed out, it looked spectacular. When he had printed out plenty, he began on the envelopes, and Amanda and Joan put the letters into the envelopes. Mark faxed the musical programme to the guests he had invited to his promotion celebration.

After lunch, Jean, the dressmaker, came to see Amanda. She was thrilled by the materials and patterns for the tops and culottes. Amanda's mum, Lady Teresa, had sent a number of different sewing threads. Jean said, "I will get on immediately."

Julian carried the mannequins and everything down for her.

Amanda told Jean, "I will be unavailable all day Thursday, and Friday morning." (Then she was to be interviewed briefly for a local-radio Christian Sunday-morning programme.)

Robert completed the differently worded letters Amanda had written, and got all these ready for posting. Mark rang the local post office and asked them to collect.

When they had gone, Amanda said, "I cannot believe it."

Robert said, "It has been teamwork." He then began transferring a design onto the cards, and trimming them. He didn't want to accept any payment. He said it had been so fulfilling, but Amanda insisted, saying, "I would like to be able to ask you again if needed."

Robert promised: "Anytime, ma'am."

Mark asked Robert, "Would you like me to ask the local police if they have a vacancy for you with your computer expertise."

Robert nearly started crying. He shook Mark's hand and said, "Thank you, sir. If it doesn't come off, you will have tried your best."

Amanda, Joan and Mark promised they would pray.

As soon as he got into his dad's car he texted to tell him that Inspector Mark had enquired about a job for him.

Brian said, "We will pray when you get home."

Robert took home a letter and place card to show his parents and told them, "Ashwood is like another world – everybody is so efficient. No wonder they have their high positions in the police force!"

Brian said, "We are very God-blessed to know them."

Mark did get Robert an interview at the local police station, six miles from home, and he obtained a position in the finance department. Part of his job involved going around the other departments, collecting and delivering information. It was a responsible job with one month's trial. After that, if satisfactory, he would attend the local college for two days per week to learn more skills in finance. His references from school and college were exemplary. His parents and grandparents were so pleased and proud that they bought him a new suit, shirts, ties and suitable shoes! Everyone at Ashwood was also very pleased.

Chapter 5

As Sandra was styling Amanda's hair before breakfast she saw Sandra was withdrawn. She gently asked her, "Are you not well or is there something you want to talk to me about?"

Sandra asked, "May I talk to you ma'am and ask your advice?"

Amanda rang Mrs Burton to ask if this was all right, and Mrs Burton told her not to get overburdened.

"No," said Amanda, "I am very fond of Sandra and would like to help, if only by listening."

She arranged for Sandra to come up to her room after breakfast whilst she was resting. They had a coffee together and Sandra said that her fiancé had been having an affair with a young woman in his office. The woman was now expecting his baby, so she had broken off the engagement.

Amanda gently asked Sandra, "Have you had sex with him?"

She replied, "No, ma'am. He kept pestering, but with my being a Christian, and in respect to my parents and family, I wanted to wait until I was married."

Amanda said, "God has given each of us free will. I am not judging anyone, but in your case I am so pleased. Well done! He obviously didn't respect you and it is better that you found out now than after you had married. Melvin agreed to wait until you were married before you became engaged. He should have honoured that. One day you will meet a young man of integrity whom you will be happy with and able to trust." She went on: "Your parents must be very proud of you."

"I suppose they are, Lady Amanda. Thank you for listening. I feel much better now."

Amanda then asked her, "What are you doing this afternoon?"

She replied, "I have three hours off as I started work at 7 a.m., ma'am."

Amanda asked her, "Would you like to go to Bryden with us?"

"Oh, yes please, ma'am. May I go to a craft shop?"

Joan said, "We are going to the one in Lissington Road. Come with us."

Mrs Burton rang the owner of the shop, Mrs Barker, to ask if there was a disabled toilet the Commander could use.

She said, "No, but the toilet is quite large – it is clean but we will go over it again."

Mrs Burton said, "We will manage, thank you."

Mrs Barker felt very honoured that the Commander was calling in.

Amanda and Joan went down to Mark and Stan, who had been walking the dogs. Amanda told them about Sandra's broken engagement and said she was coming with them that afternoon if they did not mind.

Mark said, "Well done!"

Amanda then asked, "What about Julian? I do not want to show favours."

Mark and Stan advised that he should also be asked.

Mark rang him and he accepted with joy. He asked if he could be dropped at the Rock and Roll Music Shop."

"Of course," Amanda said. "I did not know he was into rock and roll – that is interesting."

As they were travelling, they asked Julian about the rock and roll, and he said he was in a group.

Amanda said, "My boss, Commissioner Johnson, is hoping to come up for lunch soon and he is a rock-and-roll fan! When he visits, would you and your friends consider doing a session?"

Julian said, "We would be very honoured, ma'am. What does he particularly like?"

She laughed: "I have no idea, but I will ask my dada. He plays golf with the Commissioner and they often have dinner together." (Amanda, however, kept her relationship with the Commissioner strictly professional.)

Mrs Burton told them, "Sandra, Julian and his friends worship at the local Fellowship Church."

Amanda was very interested in this.

They dropped Julian off at the music shop; and Joan, Mrs Burton and Sandra went to the craft shop at the bottom of the road where Schofield's menswear shop is. Mr Schofield, the owner, was very pleased to meet the Commander. She sat comfortably in her chair and, whilst Mark was having the final fitting for the suit he was having made for the promotion morning, she chose three summer shirts each for her dada and Joshua's birthdays from the latest designs Mr Schofield had ready for her. They were very good quality. Stan bought two. Amanda asked to see the latest ties. The assistant brought a selection and Amanda also bought two for each of them. She was delighted to know that the shirts would suit their colouring and be comfortable.

Mark came out of the fitting room and they showed him their purchases.

He said, laughing, "I can't be left out of this," and Amanda picked out three shirts and three ties that would suit him. Mark laughed and told Mr Schofield, "I haven't had a lady choose my clothes since my mother when I was small."

They all laughed.

Then Mark said, "We will go to pick up the rest of our party from the craft shop."

Mr Schofield said, "We will have everything packed for you. Will you accept a glass of sherry or something when you all come back?"

"That will be very nice. Our driver is outside with the dogs." Amanda told him.

The assistant made him a coffee, and George carried water for the dogs. Then Amanda and Mark went to the craft shop.

The owners were over the moon that the Commander had come. Joan took her into the toilet.

Joan bought patterns and wool to make Amanda a bolero. She had also bought, with excitement, silk yarn and patterns – she hadn't seen a shop like this for years! Sandra bought a tablecloth and skeins; Mrs Burton bought embroidery skeins; and Amanda bought discontinued balls of wool from a basket. She would use it to knit squares to make blankets for her dog baskets. She also bought colourful offcuts for Jean to make tops for her and for Joan to use for her quilting. Joan then found a pile of 1950s knitting and sewing patterns, which Mrs Barker gave her as she had been ready to throw them out! Mrs Barker also said she would look out more patterns, odd balls of wool and scraps of material. Amanda loved the 1950s styles. The shop was like an Aladdin's cave!

Mrs Barker came outside with them, and Mark and Stan introduced themselves. She congratulated Mark on his promotion and asked them all to please come again. They said they certainly would. They thanked Mrs Barker, saying how much they had enjoyed their visit to her shop.

They went back to the menswear shop, and Mr Schofield offered them a glass of sherry each. They promised to come again. The tailor gave Mark a book of the latest suit materials – they had a duplicate. Mark thanked Mr Schofield. He put the purchases in the car and they set off. Amanda said she was looking forward to seeing Mark in his new suit.

Stan said, "I could transfer a sketch I have made of the Commander's dogs onto material for embroidering, if you like."

"We certainly would, thank you," Joan and Mrs Burton both said.

When they picked Julian up he had obtained the music he and his group needed. Everyone was happy. Sandra had cheered up, and Mrs Burton said, "Life has been so much happier since the Commander came."

Mark and the others agreed.

Joan said, "I am always happy when I am with her."

Stan asked, "Whatever are we going to do when you go back, ma'am?"

Amanda said, "Until I can work full-time, I will be coming here for long weekends. I should be able to zoom up in my helicopter."

Mark said, "I am going to kidnap her."

Amanda asked laughingly, "You and whose army?"

They all laughed.

After breakfast on Wednesday Mark and Stan took the dogs for a walk. When Amanda and Joan came down they met with the Morley chefs to discuss the wines her dada had had sent up for

Mark's lunch. They wrote the suggestions but Amanda advised, "Have some different bottles ready in case people do not like the ones we have chosen."

They said, "Yes, ma'am, we will make you proud of us."

She thanked them.

Amanda was nervous. It was the first time she had been a hostess, but she was going to try to be her natural self as she had been advised. She wanted to make sure that everyone was relaxed and enjoying themselves. She wanted to please Mark.

After lunch, Amanda and Mark went over the programme and checked the words Luke had put into the computer to be displayed on the screen. They sang and played the piano and organ, then took the dogs down to the river, then they joined Stan and Joan for afternoon tea.

Chapter 6

On Thursday Mark set off with his dad to Chesterton Police Station.

Amanda told him, "I am very proud of you."

He looked wonderful in his new clothes. He was interviewed for the local television networks – he answered questions and gave a brief insight into what his new job entailed. After the promotion ceremony they came out to be greeted by the photographers and reporters. Mark was given a bunch of red roses for the Commander, and someone called out, "Enjoy your lunch and afternoon with the Commander."

They all laughed.

When they arrived at Ashwood, those who hadn't met Amanda were overwhelmed by her beauty and charm. She immediately made them feel at ease. Then they were introduced to Reverend Brian; Hugh they knew already.

The men went to freshen up and leave their jackets. Chief Constable Blake sat on Amanda's left, Mark on her right. They all tucked into the wonderful food and questions were asked about the quality of the wines. Amanda told them where they had been produced and the type of grape as they drank them with each course. There was a very relaxed atmosphere.

Chief Constable Blake asked, "Are you settling here away from home and London?"

She told them, "Yes, and I am enjoying my exercise programme, but the swimming is the best benefit to me just now."

Mark told them about her exercise programme in London and her SAS training. They all said she put them to shame, and they all vowed 'to pull their socks up'.

Bob told them, "The Commander is a high-kicker!"

She said, "Not at the moment!"

He told them about the Morecambe and Wise sketch, and they all said they would like to see it.

She told them, "The programme is being broadcast soon. When it first was due to be shown the London bombings took place so it was postponed."

They said, "Of course."

"I am very thankful that ITV honoured my charity by giving them the fee they promised me for taking part. It has been put to very good use."

The Chief Constable asked about her 140-mph chase.

She said, "I just prayed I wouldn't run out of petrol!" She told them about the Italian she had nicked – he had told the police how much he admired her spirit and promised he would go straight in future. "I found out he had just married, for the fourth time, to a karate-trained woman and she had threatened him with what she would do if he broke the law again."

They all laughed.

Amanda went on: "It is hard not to like some of the criminals: do you find this so?"

They agreed.

Chief Inspector Sykes asked, "Do you have a liking for Italians?"

"Yes, my mum is Italian. I adore her, of course, and my dada and I absolutely adore my aunt, Contessa Sophie."

He then asked, "Do you speak Italian?"

Mark answered, "Fluently."

Amanda asked, "Apart from Mark, does anyone speak Italian?"

A few did and spoke out. She answered them and encouraged Mark to join in.

Inspector Carter asked, "How do you stay calm whilst interviewing? Do you ever get angry?"

She said, "Of course, but I don't show it. They know how far they can go with me. I have learned to control my face muscles."

They asked her to show her favourite technique.

Mark and the others moved to the other side of the table.

"I relax my eyes as though I am engrossed with every breath and word they are saying," she said, "then I relax my mouth as though I believe them. When they finish their lies they think I have been taken in, but I say to them, 'Oh, really?' pause, 'You are nicked.' Usually they burst out laughing!"

They asked, "Any more?"

"No, because I may have to arrest you lot."

They asked, "Arrest us?" and great laughter went round the table.

They were enjoying her company and said they had never enjoyed a lunch and fellowship more.

She thanked them.

She was then asked how much she and her dada had won on *Celebrity Charity Quiz*?

She told them, "We are not allowed to say, but we did our best. It will be broadcast a week Saturday evening. The surviving members of my team are coming up that weekend. I am in one way dreading it because I will be looking for the ones who were killed." She broke down a little at that, and they waited for her to recover. "Also, I only know the ones who are coming professionally."

They assured her she would make them feel comfortable, in the same way as she had made them feel during lunch.

She thanked them.

One of the officers suggested, "If you do not mind me saying, Commander, you ought to let them know how broken you are about the ones killed."

"Thank you. Yes, I will at the appropriate time. It will be a healing and learning time for every one of us – and, thankfully, Mark, Joan, Inspector Stan will be with me. Chief Inspector Hawkins is also my great friend."

They thought Bob had retired: "He is always missing since you came, but he has earned time off. He isn't neglecting anything; besides, he has always put work first."

Chief Constable Blake then said, "You appear to be getting on well with Mark."

She told them, "He is horrible, terrible, bossing me about!" then burst out laughing.

They all joined in.

After Amanda was asked her programme when she returned to

the Met, she told them, "I cannot plan anything until I know the next treatment for my knee. When I am well enough I will return part-time, but relegated to my desk."

"Will you like that?"

"No, I like to be in action with my team. I will live with my beloved family and animals during the week and return here for long weekends. I should be able to travel up in my helicopter."

"You have a helicopter?"

"Yes, I use it often in London. My fiancé's parents bought it for us as an engagement present. When he was killed, I decided to keep it. Also I have the car Andrew made extra-safe for me; he adored building up old cars in his spare time. He was a wonderful man. I knew him for twenty-one years."

Joan agreed.

Chief Constable Blake asked, "Eventually, will you marry?"

Amanda asked him, "Are you proposing?"

They all laughed and then she nudged him and mimicked in a Dick Emery voice, "Ooh, you are orful, but I like you!"

They were all amazed and Joan told them, "She is a right mimic, but only in a kindly way."

Mark said, "I didn't know."

Whilst they were eating their dessert, Julian came and apologised for interrupting. "Ma'am, Commissioner Johnson is on your secure line to speak urgently to you."

Amanda asked the table, "May I?" After greeting the Commissioner she listened intently and then burst out laughing and said, "Thank you, sir. I pray everything goes as scheduled."

He then asked, "You are at lunch celebrating the Chief Superintendent's promotion?"

"Yes, sir."

"I would like to come up to Ashwood for lunch with you. I hopefully have a few days' leave in three weeks – perhaps I could come up then with your dada and mum?"

"You will be very welcome, sir. We have a local rock-and-roll group, sir, so we could have a musical afternoon. Be in touch later. Bye, sir."

She told them, "The Commissioner has invited himself up for lunch with my dada and mum in three weeks when hopefully he has a few days' leave."

They all said, "Wow!"

"Will you be able to come to meet him and make him feel welcome?"

They all said, "We will pull out all the stops for this."

Amanda then said, "I am talking too much – it is Mark's lunch."

Mark and all of them asked, "Please continue. We have never been so entertained."

"Right," she said, "the Commissioner rang because we have had a breakthrough in a drugs case I am working on. The Met have received inside information and hundreds of arrests are being made this afternoon. It will be on the news. Also, they are breaking into a mansion in London. This is a fortress, so special equipment has had to be brought in to get through windows and inner doors."

They asked, "Would you have been in this?"

"No, the toughest specially trained men and the SAS are carrying out this operation. I am part of the team working behind the scenes."

"Does the Commissioner ring you often?"

"Yes, he keeps me in touch."

"He must be missing you."

"We have a professional relationship. I admire him greatly – he is a wonderful leader."

"Is he married?"

"No."

Senior Inspector Marshall promised, "I will put extra security on when the Commissioner comes. How will he travel?"

"Most likely, by police helicopter."

Inspector Stan told them, "The Commander has arranged for me to have her fiancé's old cars to do up when I retire."

"Yes," said Amanda, "that was God's timing. When he and Chief Inspector Hawkins came to lunch last Friday, I asked Inspector Stan if he has any hobbies for when he retires. He told us about his wanting to get an old car to rebuild. I rang Andrew's parents to ask about the cars Andrew had, and – what do you think? – they were going to ring me that very afternoon – we keep in close contact – with the news that they are retiring to Portugal. I know they love it there, as they have been there for holidays and a lot of their friends have retired or are retiring there.

They hadn't told me before, as Ian said they wanted me to get stronger. I said I had rung enquiring about Andrew's cars. Ian – bless him! – asked if I wanted them. I told him I know someone who does, who will love them and take care of them. He was very thankful. He and Georgina had been wondering what to do with them. They didn't want them to go to the wrong home. So, they have arranged transport and the cars will arrive tomorrow – four to the local garage and two here."

They all said, "Wow! He would have been so pleased."

They asked, "What makes are they?"

Amanda said, "I want them to be a surprise for Stan, Inspector."

They urged her to tell them, and Stan also said, "Yes please – I can't wait for them."

"OK, a 1950s Morris Minor, a 1960s Morris Minor police car, a very old burgundy Austin, a 1970s Triumph Stag, an MGTC Midget and a 1953 Morris Traveller."

They were all struck dumb.

Amanda went on: "Miss Joan is having one."

They told her she had done well to remember the makes.

Mark informed them, "The Commander has an IQ of 160."

They all said, "We would love to see them. When may we come again?"

Amanda suggested, "Come before my chief's visit, but I am going to be tied up next week."

They asked, "Are you going to tell us?"

"Mark doesn't know yet," she answered.

Mark asked her, "Please tell all of us."

"Right," she said. "This morning, Dougie Hamilton rang asking me to give him a one-hour interview for his Friday-night programme before *Celebrity Charity Quiz*." Looking at Mark, she added, "I said I would because what I will say will help a lot of people. I have to prepare suggestions for questions for him to ask, and provide photographs and videos. He and his crew are coming up to the Morley next Wednesday and they will film on Thursday morning to be broadcast, as I have said, on Friday night."

Bob asked, "It is usually a half-hour programme."

"Yes, but this will be one-hour; Dougie wants me to sing."

"Right. We appreciate you will be out of action."

"Once I have got it together and faxed him, everything will fall into place."

Reverend Brian gave thanks for the wonderful meal and fellowship. He prayed for Amanda's interview to be successful and for a continuation of the healing of her cramps. The Chief Constable congratulated Mark on his promotion and thanked Amanda for the beautiful lunch and for entertaining them. They all clapped. Amanda texted Mrs Burton to ask the chefs and all who had waited on them to come to be thanked. They came and were clapped and thanked. Photographs were then taken of the table and all of them.

Amanda and Joan went upstairs and the men went to the pool lounge. They all met up outside, where more photographs and videos were taken.

They went inside for the musical entertainment, to which the staff, press and reporters had also been invited. Amanda sang, as requested, 'You'll Never Walk Alone', and she played whilst Mark sang 'Here's to the Heroes'. They went through a marvellous programme.

Then, with Mark playing on the organ, they had a community sing-song. The words were projected onto a screen – 'Now Thank We All Our God' and a rousing 'Praise My Soul, the King of Heaven'. Everyone sang with gusto. It was a perfect end to the afternoon. Luke prepared videos of the afternoon for the guests to share with their families, and Bob arranged for a patrol car to deliver them. Mark's summary of what his new job entailed and video clips of the afternoon were shown on the local television networks, and his summary and photographs were in the local papers and magazines.

Amanda thanked Mrs Burton and told her that Dougie and crew would be coming up to the Morley and having lunch here on Thursday.

"Will you ask the chefs to cook this?" she said, handing Mrs Burton a menu.

Amanda later rang the Morley and told them that in three weeks her chief and her parents would be coming up for lunch. Amanda then suggested that her mum's Italian chef could come to help.

"Will you be able to put him and his assistant up on Thursday evening? Separate rooms – his assistant is a female!"

The chefs were very excited at this news.

"This will be arranged, ma'am."

Amanda rang her mum and told her about the interview. She asked her to send her photograph albums and any other photographs and videos she had suitable for her interview with Duggie Hamilton. "Also, Mum, Commissioner Johnson is coming up to lunch in three weeks' time. When we know the day, will you and Dada please come with him in his helicopter? May I borrow Marcos also, please, Mum?"

Lady Teresa said she was so proud of her daughter and she said she would text her dada to tell him and ask him if he could arrange a few days' holiday around the time of the lunch. "We will send you plenty of wines and anything else. I will ask Marcos now to make sure he will not be on holiday."

Amanda and Mark sat outside having a cup of tea and she told him what she had just arranged with her mum.

Mark said, "Whilst you and Joan are organising the interview I will do some work on my laptop. This will leave me free later to spend time with you. We will still be able to swim as usual. Thank you for everything, Amanda. It has been so wonderful today; everyone is so encouraged and uplifted. They say you are like a breath of fresh air. They don't want you to return to the Met."

Pangs of despair went through Mark every time Amanda mentioned going back to work.

Stan and Joan had taken the dogs down to the river whilst they had time alone to discuss the day.

The local Christian radio presenter came at 10.30 on Friday morning to record the interview for Sunday morning. Amanda sang, with her guitar, 'Be Thou My Vision', and said how comfortable she was, living in this area. She thanked everyone for their welcome and said she was very pleased she was getting to know them better.

The presenter asked, "Was your faith shaken recently when your knee was shattered and the members of your team were killed – also when your fiancé Andrew was killed four years ago?"

"No, there is no darkness in God, only light. He abhors violence. Of course I have doubts, but was there anything I could have done to prevent the attack? It had been a totally unexpected attack, but if we had had sniffer dogs with us, possibly it might have been prevented. This is a lesson for us. I am going all out to provide more dogs and handlers, and I am setting up a charity for this purpose."

"How are the dogs at Ashwood, ma'am?"

"Hero and Storm have made it – they were used in London a few days ago. They are marvellous at sniffing out bombs, explosives, drugs, etc. Cambridge and Oxford will not go back to that work. I have bought them, and when they are stronger they will be put to stud and I pray that their puppies will be able to be trained." Amanda said, "Being in the police isn't easy these days. The police need community support and they are worth every penny they receive. They put their lives at risk to keep the public safe."

She then answered questions about her knee. She said she was going back to hospital after the month was up, and prayed that the muscle tissues would have healed enough for further treatment.

"After being so active, it must be irksome?"

"Yes, it was at first, but I am adjusting and am so thankful for the expert help I receive. My brother and his wife released Miss Joan to look after me. She was my nanny, and I have Miss Biggin during the night. My best exercise is swimming."

"And now Chief Superintendent Young is with you at Ashwood to help you with your therapy?"

"Yes. Before he begins his new job. I needed someone I felt safe with to take me swimming – especially as I get cramp. I do thank God these attacks of cramp are getting fewer now. I am using the muscles as best I can with the brace."

"If you were to fall or slip, would this be disastrous, Commander?"

"Yes."

"We thank you, Commander, for giving us this interview. May we ask you to give us another soon, please?"

"Yes, I will be delighted. When my knee is sorted I will be working at the Met part-time – during the week to begin with, and coming up to Ashwood for weekends. I should be able to travel in my helicopter."

Amanda had previously asked if she could finish with 'Praise

My Soul, the King of Heaven' from a CD of the local Brookwell Male Voice Choir.

Everyone was delighted with this encouraging interview. Requests were received for more of the Commander and listeners phoned in to ask where they could buy the CD.

Mark asked Amanda, "Would you like to go to The Open Church this Sunday morning?"

She said, "Love to."

He told Matthew, the vicar, this news.

Matthew was pleased and said everyone else would be too.

Mark warned Matthew, "With it being further than St James', and because of the dogs' routine, it will be 11 a.m. before we arrive – that is, traffic allowing."

Matthew said, "We will pray, do the business and then listen to the Brookwell Choir CD until you come."

The Open Church was large. They had a music group, and colourful posters were all round the walls. Mark and Stan told Amanda and Joan that they had a wonderful big youth group and that the 6.30 p.m. services were led by them. The youths also met during the week to take part in different activities.

Everyone was pleased to meet Amanda and Joan. Matthew was coming back with them for lunch. They had met him previously at Mark's lunch. He was tall, very good looking, and single.

When he and Amanda were on their own, he asked her, "Will you please give me an opportunity to take you somewhere for a meal?" He said, "I am asking before others do."

Amanda was angry, but tried to disguise it. She told him in her Commander voice, "Reverend Matthew, thank you but I haven't come here to find a man. My beloved fiancé was killed four years ago and I am still grieving for him."

He apologised.

Mark came rushing up – he had noticed the negative body language.

To cover up, Amanda smiled at him and said, " I have enjoyed the service."

Matthew admitted he had unknowingly upset her, and he said he would pass the message on that ma'am was still grieving for her fiancé.

Mark wasn't pleased, but he understood. 'She is so beautiful,' he said to himself.

Amanda, with her breeding and training, put Matthew at ease and talked with him about his sermon.

Matthew later apologised to Mark for upsetting Amanda. He told Mark what he had asked and said ruefully, "You can tell she is a commander. If she wasn't handicapped by her damaged leg, I would have been in real trouble."

Mark told him, "She is emotional, coming to terms with what had recently happened, meeting me, and my connection with Andrew. This is a different world to her – away from her family and home, away from the Met."

Matthew apologised again. He said he had never met anyone like her and wanted to be in her company.

Mark told him, "Be relaxed with her and she will often invite you and other Christian friends. Your mistake was to ask her whilst she was on her own; it should have been when Miss Joan or I was with her."

Brian, Hugh and their families also came to lunch.

Afterwards Matthew said to Amanda, "Mark will be a wonderful chief superintendent."

She agreed.

Chapter 7

On Thursday breakfast was at 7 a.m. Amanda could only eat fruit and toast as she was nervous. Mark, Joan and Stan prayed with her for a successful interview. Mark said Dougie had been brought to the Morley in a helicopter.

Dougie and the crew arrived at 8.30 and Amanda joined them at 9.30 in her chair with Sparky and Champion. The make-up girl compensated for the effect of the lights.

Dougie asked, "Ready, Commander?"

She took a deep breath, remembering her training in how to cope in stressful situations. The programme opened with Amanda singing 'Be Thou My Vision', which she had recorded with Mark. Whilst this was playing, films and photographs were shown of Amanda riding her horse, Tarquin, on the Sussex Downs; of her with Thunder, her Rottweiler; of Andrew working on his car; of him and Amanda walking with their arms round each other with their horses; of her accompanying her dada playing the violin; of her walking in the garden with her mum and all the dogs. She was shown climbing ropes with the SAS (their faces obscured); laying a wreath on Remembrance Day at the Cenotaph; standing to attention with the Commissioner; greeting the Queen at an official opening; at the Pavarotti concerts with the Contessa; being carried on her stretcher to Ashwood; with Joan, Mark and Stan at Ashwood; going in her chair down to the river with them and the dogs; walking with her sticks; swimming with Mark; playing computer tennis (also with him); playing the piano; and hosting the lunch for Mark.

Dougie asked, "How are you?"

Amanda answered, "I am being greatly cared for by my ex-nanny, Miss Joan; my night nurse, Miss Biggin; Superintendent Young and his father; all the Ashwood staff; and the chefs from the Morley. I am very grateful to Chief Inspector Hawkins for his help and kindness." (At this point a photograph of the Chief Inspector was shown.) "I am enjoying being with the people in the community."

Dougie said, "Your parents are amazed how you have settled. They greatly miss you."

Amanda replied, "I miss my parents and family but would have felt stifled at home or in a private nursing home – although, I must confess, at first I didn't settle. The transition from being super-active to having my nurses attending to all my physical needs was a difficult one."

He asked, "Would it be a disaster if you slipped or fell?"

"Yes."

"Then what happened, ma'am?"

"I asked for a Christian person to help me with my swimming therapy, who shared my interests (especially in music) and loved dogs. Inspector Young came. He was having a few days' holiday before his promotion. Chief Superintendent Mark had been my fiancé's colonel in Afghanistan when Andrew and two of his colleagues were killed. My parents will be horrified when I tell you that, in spite of my being terribly well brought up, and in spite of my training in the Met, and in spite of being a practising Christian, I was so angry and hurt that I blamed him for neglect.

"Unknown to my parents and family, I stopped him coming to Andrew's funeral. I have been so busy these last four years that there have been only odd moments when I have remembered him, but when the members of my team were killed I realised how absolutely wicked and unfair I had been to this man.

"Andrew had told me he lived in this area, so when I came here I tried to contact him through security. I drew a blank, but the authorities informed him I was trying to get in touch with him. He contacted me and made an appointment to see me. When he arrived, my dogs, which are trained to be wary of strangers, went potty with delight over him! He explained that he now worked for the local police, since his time in Afghanistan was over. I told him how sorry I was for my behaviour. How could I have been so cruel? I should have been supporting him in his ordeal. He told me he understood. I had known Andrew for twenty-one years, but he had also been devastated at the time." (At this point photographs were shown of Amanda and Andrew growing up.) "Mark said he would be happy to help me and that he had welcomed the opportunity to communicate with me. I said, 'Yes, please,' he stayed for lunch and moved into his room, which had been prepared. Unknown to me, he gave up his holiday in Italy and his chance of seeing a Pavarotti concert. Another thing I didn't know was that at another time he was at one of these concerts when I was there. I didn't know what he looked like at the time, but he saw me.

"I am so pleased that God directed me here. We are now the best of friends, and we both share the same interests. He is a wonderful Christian man. Not only was he able to forgive and forget when he had been hurt, but, unknown to me, he was in monthly contact with my parents, asking how I was. He also keeps in contact with the bereaved of the other two soldiers killed with Andrew. My parents were delighted when he came here; they know he is a man of integrity. Through this, Dougie, I can appreciate people being angry when their loved ones are killed or injured. It isn't easy for the bereaved, but I pray that what I have said will help to increase understanding for those in similar situations. It's very hard."

Dougie then mentioned, "Lady Cynthia went to Italy in your place?"

"Yes, my aunt, the Contessa, cannot travel now with her heart condition, and she admits she should not smoke [photo of Amanda as small girl holding her nose and saying, 'Oo smell, Aunty'] but there we are. I adore her. Chief Superintendent Mark has set up a computer camera link with Aunt Sophie, which is wonderful. We can see one another as we talk. She is very frail now. I will get to her as soon as possible. I am very thankful that Lady Cynthia is with her and they are able to go to some of the concerts."

"Your fiancé, Andrew – did he share your love of music?"

"No," laughed Amanda, "his passion was building up old cars [photo of Andrew with car]. He built me one up – it is at home.

52

He and the members of my team who died will always live on in my heart."

Amanda broke down. Her dogs whimpered and licked her, then they turned on Dougie, growling and showing their teeth. He stood up – the crew were laughing.

Amanda in a stern voice said, "Sit!"

The dogs sat, and so did Dougie. The crew were doubled up with laughter, and Amanda and Dougie joined in.

"Are you all right to continue, ma'am?"

"Yes, Dougie, are you?"

Everyone laughed again, and Amanda had a drink of water.

Dougie said, "You had known Andrew since you were three?"

"Yes. He was a friend of my brother Joshua."

Dougie then said he had been informed that when Amanda was only three years old several of Joshua's friends wouldn't come when she was at home – they rang first.

Amanda laughed. "Yes, I was a pain – I used to throw them about."

Everyone laughed.

"Now you are SAS-trained?"

"Yes, even though I'm handicapped with my brace just now, I have skills that would put anyone out of action."

"Had you a date for your wedding, ma'am?"

"No, we just drifted along, I suppose. After Andrew was killed I had doubts and questions – should I have known him fully?"

Dougie asked, "What do you mean?"

Amanda replied, "We were engaged, but Andrew respected my wish to be a virgin until we were married before God."

He asked in amazement, "You are a virgin, ma'am?"

"Yes," she replied, "I am untouched. I had great consolation when my brother told me Andrew had said virginity is the greatest gift a bride can give her husband. This comforted me."

"Commander, have you played and sung with Pavarotti?"

"Yes," she replied laughing, "at dinner parties the Contessa gave for him [photo]. After Andrew's funeral Pavarotti told us Andrew had asked him to compile a CD of him singing some of my favourites. When he gave me the CD, my heart behaved strangely. To me it was confirmation that he had been thankful

I had my music so he could get on with his cars. This arrangement worked very well – we never fell out. I shall never forget that evening – it is embossed in my heart."

Dougie said, "A wonderful man!"

Amanda replied, "A wonderful Christian man!"

"After the music, did Pavarotti go home?"

"No, he played bridge."

"Did you, ma'am?"

"No, I went swimming in the private lake at the back of the villa. Miss Joan used to come with me when possible. At the side of the lake there is a cave where we collected pieces of wood before we swam, and afterwards we would make a fire in the cave. Then we sang at the top of our voices."

"Did they hear you at the villa?"

"No one has said," laughed Amanda. "We were a fair way off."

Dougie asked, "What happened to Andrew's cars?"

"That is another God-blessed thing. I rang Andrew's parents – I am in constant touch with them, and we love each other – and Lord Ian was on the point of ringing me. There is nothing unusual about that, but it was to tell me they had made arrangements that very morning to sell their home and buy a house in Portugal. They had waited until I was a little stronger before they told me. I knew some friends of theirs lived in Portugal and enjoyed holidays there. I told Ian I had rung him to ask about Andrew's cars and parts. He asked if I wanted them. They were wondering what to do with them. I asked if it was possible for a friend who was retiring to have them, and they agreed. They sent everything to us. Miss Joan is having one of the cars. Andrew would be so pleased that these old cars will live on. God certainly works in mysterious ways."

"How are the sniffer dogs, ma'am? [photo] Hero and Storm are OK, but Cambridge and Oxford are not 100%. I have bought them, and when they are strong enough I will have them put them to stud. Then I pray that the puppies can be trained. I am an advocate for more sniffer dogs. I want to see more and more trained. If my team and I had had one with us, we might have avoided the killings and the injury to my knee. I am not blaming anyone, Dougie: it was a vicious unexpected attack, but I want the authorities to be aware of this vital need in this day and age. I am going to set up a charity to buy more dogs and employ more trainers."

"Yes, ma'am, I can see you will not let this rest."

Amanda shook her head.

"You must be missing your horse, Tarquin, and Thunder, your Rottweiler?"

"Yes, I made a video to greet them morning and evening so they won't miss me altogether. They must laugh, thinking, 'Here she is again.' We forget animals have brains [photo of Tarquin and Thunder looking up at the video]."

The crew laughed.

"Ma'am, are you a friend of the royal family?"

"I have that honour [photo of Amanda with them enjoying a barbecue at Balmoral, and then she and the Queen out riding and talking]. These photographs are shown with Her Majesty's approval."

"Your brother, Joshua, has a share in Mason's of London?"

"Yes, Joshua was Aunt Melissa's heir. He is a sleeping partner. I am Contessa Sophie's heiress."

"What will this entail, ma'am?"

"I will inherit her one-third share in Mason's and, with my mum and my brother, my aunt's villa in Italy."

Dougie asked, "How did you react when your knee was shattered, ma'am?"

"I confess there are times when I get impatient with what I cannot do physically. I wake up and start to jump out of bed, then I realise."

"What is the prognosis for your knee, Commander?"

"We cannot tell until the brace comes off. At least I am alive and I have my leg."

"You used your Taser in the attack, Commander?"

"Yes, my reaction was to use both the Taser and my revolver. I am appealing for more Tasers to be used. They put people out of action so that they may be overcome, and they avoid fatal mistakes."

"Will you return to the Met part-time to begin with?"

"Yes. It will be desk work."

"How will you react to this, Commander?"

"A commander can command from a desk, but I like to be in action with my team. The remaining members of my team are coming up tomorrow. I shall be very glad to see them."

Dougie then said, "You and your dada's *Celebrity Charity Quiz* will be broadcast tomorrow evening?"

"Yes, we did our best. It is so different being in the studio – it looks easy at home."

"Your charity is for children and teenagers in East London who are in desperate need."

"My brother and I had such a wonderful secure childhood [photos of Amanda's mum cuddling her and Joshua, her dada with arms wide open to embrace them, their parents playing games with them, and Amanda playing the piano at eight years old with her dada playing the violin]. We were not spoilt – we had to earn our pocket money [photos of Amanda and Joshua scrubbing wellingtons, bathing dogs, grooming their ponies, and collecting firewood and eggs]. There are two things I abhor: cruelty to children and cruelty to animals. Every child and animal deserves to be loved and cared for, to feel secure. With the help of dedicated volunteers, who give their time freely, we give children camping holidays in the country. This teaches them to be self-sufficient. They do enjoy themselves, especially when they are able to swim in a river. I cannot praise these volunteer carers enough. They encourage these teenagers to live wholesome Christian lives and to stay out of trouble. They keep them occupied with activities. They are taught that the world does not owe them a living – they have to apply themselves. They are encouraged to work hard at school, and to treat themselves and everyone they meet with respect. We have been greatly encouraged by results."

"Your dada's charity is for families who are victims of crime, including the families of convicted criminals?"

"Yes, dada is absolutely committed to this cause."

"Ma'am, you also did a sketch for *The Morecambe and Wise Show*?"

Laughing, Amanda said, "Yes, it wasn't shown – it wasn't appropriate with the London bombings – but it is going to be shown soon."

"You did some high kicks?"

"Yes, but I cannot do them just now. I was very grateful when ITV agreed to pay my fee to my charity; it was put to very good use [clip of Amanda kicking off Ernie's hat]."

Dougie then asked, "Have you thought of living in Italy, Commander?"

"I love Italy – the people, and of course because the Contessa is there. I go whenever I can to be with my aunt, but my work is in London. I am trained to be a commander."

Dougie said, "There is talk about you being promoted, ma'am?"

Amanda sternly said, "We will not go there."

He laughed. "Point taken, ma'am."

"Will you marry?"

"Dougie, are you proposing?"

They all laughed.

"Is there anyone on the horizon?"

Amanda said, "You are like a dog chewing a bone."

He answered, "That's why I am a presenter, ma'am."

She nodded.

After they had finished they had a drink, then Amanda went upstairs with Joan. Mark took Dougie and the crew to the pool lounge.

Amanda went back in and they ran through the film. She and Dougie made a few alterations. The crew arranged to have their lunch before they spliced together the videos and photographs.

Dougie joined Amanda, Joan, Mark and Stan and told them, "I have never enjoyed an interview more. If only every one was so easy."

They had good fellowship during the meal and Amanda felt at ease. Dougie said he would like to end the interview with Amanda singing again. Amanda and Mark asked if 'You'll Never Walk Alone' might be suitable, and they seized on that.

Mark suggested they could film Amanda playing her piano and singing, and then she could be filmed outside on her own supported with her sticks, looking out thoughtfully with the dogs.

Dougie was over the moon at this. The cameramen were also thrilled by the idea of this ending. Later they showed the almost completed interview to Amanda and Dougie.

Dougie asked Amanda, "Will you give me another interview at a later date?"

She told him, "With pleasure!"

It was good. Dougie asked if they could show clips in the news for publicity. The programme had been publicised on television and in the papers since the Wednesday as a one-hour special.

Amanda said, "Whatever you think is appropriate."

They packed up their equipment and had a quick drink before rushing back to London to complete the film. They agreed to send a copy to Amanda for the following morning. The helicopter arrived at the Morley to take Dougie back for his Thursday programme.

Amanda and her gang sat outside with a glass of beer each. They congratulated her on how she had sailed through the day. They were very proud of her.

She told them, "I have greatly enjoyed the challenge, and I pray that what I have said will help to bring about better understanding." She then said, "I'm not sure whether to watch the film tomorrow afternoon or wait until the evening television presentation."

They said, "Please let us see it."

Bob rang then to ask how it went.

Mark said, "Everything has gone according to plan. I knew it would."

Amanda asked Mark if Bob could come for lunch the next day and see a preview.

He replied, "Try to keep me away," and he worked overtime to make up for the time he would miss.

Lady Teresa then rang and was reassured that Amanda was OK. Dougie and the crew were happy. Amanda's mum told her how proud she and her dada were. She said she would fax the Contessa's housekeeper whilst Amanda relaxed. Mark and Amanda prepared for their swim.

On the news, clips were shown of Amanda saying how Andrew and the members of her team would always live on in her heart, of her breaking down, of the dogs comforting her, of her singing

'You'll Never Walk Alone' and of Dougie saying he had never enjoyed an interview more.

On Friday after breakfast Amanda and Mark had their swim while Stan took the dogs for their usual walk. Bob came and they all enjoyed lunch. Amanda was a little nervous about the film, but they all settled with the dogs and Mark set the film going.

They were enthralled; it was so professional! There were only two advertisements breaks – one for dog food, and the other for computer games! They all fell about laughing at Amanda as she commanded the dogs to sit and Dougie also obeyed! Amanda faxed Dougie, congratulating and thanking him and the crew.

Bob asked, "May we see it again?"

They said they would after a drink and break.

Mark rang Mrs Burton: "Would you like to see the Commander's interview?"

She also rang Sandra and Julian, but told them to keep it confidential until the evening.

Afterwards they all congratulated her. Amanda rang her mum and faxed the Contessa's housekeeper.

Amanda asked, "Bob, are you having dinner with us?"

"Yes, please."

They decided to eat together as Adam was coming for the first time. Amanda and Mark usually had dinner on their own and conversed in Italian.

Stan and Bob went to fetch Adam from the railway station. He was so excited at meeting the Commander and coming to Ashwood. He had created some beautiful illustrations for Amanda's letterheads and quarter-fold cards.

Everyone was so pleased to meet him; he rushed up and greeted Amanda, thanking her for making them all happy. "You are beautiful, ma'am. May I send a photograph of you to my uni friends?" He then asked for a photo of himself with his arm around her shoulder."

She laughingly agreed.

Mark hugged him. Miss Biggin came and they had a wonderful meal. Then they prepared for the 8.30 interview. Mrs Burton had been invited again.

There were more close-ups of Amanda. She looked natural and gorgeous – they were all enthralled again.

Luke and Adam had to sleep at home as all the other rooms were being decorated, but they came back for breakfast and stayed for the day.

Mark asked Adam if he would man the telephone and computer to receive any messages whilst Luke and their dad went to fetch Amanda's guests from the railway station.

"With pleasure," he replied.

He recorded all the messages of congratulation and pledges to the Commander's charity.

ITV asked if the Commander would give more recorded interviews in their discussion programmes. The local radio requested another interview on their Sunday-morning Christian programme; another Sunday-morning Christian radio programme also requested a recorded interview.

Dougie and his crew sent the most beautiful bouquet of flowers with their thanks. Security was given messages to pass on to the Commander.

After the interview the computer company rang Ashwood to ask Amanda and Mark if they could use in an advertisement the scene of them playing computer tennis as they believed this would encourage people in wheelchairs. After Amanda, her dada and Mark had discussed it, they agreed and they announced that their fee would go to buy computers and games for disabled groups in the area. This was a great blessing.

Chapter 8

On Saturday morning Stan and Luke fetched Cheryl, Sharon, Helen, Stephen and Peter from the railway station. They were staying at the Morley – Amanda's treat.

They ran up to Amanda and they all, and Amanda, burst out crying. They put their arms around one another.

Amanda kept saying, "I am so sorry!"

Mrs Burton, Sandra and Julian came and they ordered drinks.

The team asked, "May we see your leg, ma'am?"

Amanda asked them how they were; they went quiet.

"Commander," said Helen, "please do not think me rude but I love your new hairstyle – I hardly recognise you out of uniform."

They all agreed. Joan continued knitting; Mark sat relaxed but observing.

After they had settled, Amanda asked, "What would you like to do this afternoon? You needn't stay with me if you don't want to. The dog handlers will run you anywhere."

They asked Amanda, "What are you doing?"

She said, "I have swimming therapy with Chief Superintendent Mark."

They asked, "May we join in?"

"Of course, if that is what you prefer. I can only swim briefly as I still get cramp – but not as much as I did, thank God. [They knew, of course, that she was a Christian.] Right, so after lunch shall we take the dogs down to the river first?"

"Oh yes, that will be lovely."

At lunch Adam said, "I am going with my dad and Luke to look at the old cars, if that is all right with you, ma'am?"

"Of course. Please do what you want."

Stephen asked, "May I be excused to go with them – if it is OK?"

They said, "Of course."

Peter asked, "May I also go?"

"Please do – what about you, girls?"

"Would you mind, ma'am?"

"Of course not. We want you to have a wonderful weekend. Two cars are here and the other four are in the local garage for now."

Mark said, "I will arrange transport." (He was secretly glad he would be swimming with Amanda on her own.) "Will you be going straight away after lunch?"

"If that is OK?"

"Of course."

They had a wonderful meal, and everyone relaxed. They discussed Dougie's interview: "We thought it excellent. What a wonderful singer and musician you are, ma'am!"

When they had set off, Amanda started laughing and said, "Well, I know where I am with them – they prefer not to be in my company."

"It isn't that," said Joan: "they have to get used to you not being in uniform and not being in command in a work situation."

Mark agreed. "You would feel the same if you went to the Commissioner's home and were invited to go swimming with him."

"Heaven forbid!" said Amanda. "I avoid him when he comes to my parents, but I realise now that he must have guessed I am avoiding him."

They all laughed.

Mark said, "You are doing the correct thing."

They all met up for dinner. They had had a wonderful afternoon, and they wanted the cars!

Peter said, "I will get an old car and renovate it."

Stephen said, "Me too."

The girls offered: "We will help if wanted."

Amanda said, "Good!"

Sharon told them, "Travelling up we realised we didn't really know one another well, despite working together. We are going to meet socially with some of the others in future. It will not affect our work, Commander."

Amanda reassured them: "I know that. You are most trustworthy."

Whilst Amanda went upstairs with Joan, the others went down to the river with the dogs. They thought Ashwood was great!

Later they settled in front of the TV for *Celebrity Charity Quiz*. Miss Biggin joined them. Amanda had such a surprise: Dougie introduced the programme with tributes from the Commissioner. (The team said, "Wow!") There were also tributes from SAS members (not shown), politicians, then the Queen! (Amanda went to Balmoral every September and she met up often with the royal family.)

Then Amanda walked on arm in arm with her dada, and she jumped into the chair. They all laughed, then no one moved.

Craig asked, "What charities are you supporting?"

Amanda replied, "The disadvantaged children and teenagers in East London."

The Judge told him, "I support the families of victims of crime and the families of prisoners, when they are in need."

The questions! They struggled with one which should have been simple, but the audience confirmed their right answer. The team could see they were well supported. They reached £1,000.

Craig asked them, "How are you?"

They said they were terrified, and that they never imagined it would be so nerve-racking. They thought it was easier answering the questions at home!"

He laughed.

They went up to £100,000, and Craig warned them they would lose if they gave the wrong answer at this stage.

They understood.

He talked briefly to them about their professional lives and the charities they supported.

They reached £500,000, so the next question was for £1 million! They had used all their lifelines. The question was a very difficult science question.

The Judge said to Amanda, "You will know this."

She answered, "There are two possibilities – I think this is a trick question."

Craig just sat looking at her. The Judge said, "Amanda darling, trust your first instinct."

"I wouldn't hesitate but I am afraid I will lose all that money for our charities." She closed her eyes in prayer. Then she answered.

For a moment, Craig just looked at her, giving nothing away – then pandemonium broke out! Balloons, streamers, everybody on their feet: they had won.

Amanda hugged her dada and shook Craig's hand. Her mum came with brother Joshua, his wife, Nicola, and even three-year-old Susan. They all hugged one another and cried.

Some of the disadvantaged teenagers came. They stood grinning into the camera. Three leaders shook her hand, and the hands of Andrew's parents. Everybody continued clapping and cheering, and there were camera flashes all over the place. Susan clung on to Amanda's leg until she lifted her up and kissed her.

All at Ashwood were cheering.

The team said, "What a beautiful family you have!"

Miss Biggin said, "Isn't your dada handsome?"

Bob said, "Your mum is a beauty too!"

"I agree, and my brother and Nicola are also gorgeous."

Julian and Sandra brought champagne in, and they and Mrs Burton joined everyone else in a glass, saying how wonderful it had been.

Peter asked, "How did you keep that quiet, Commander?"

Helen replied, "It is ma'am's training."

Mark was thrilled. He said, "We are very proud of you."

She asked him, "Did you know the answer?"

"It was extremely difficult. It could have been either of the options."

The phone rang, and the dogs chased about all over the place. Luke went to answer. People were ringing in their congratulations.

Sharon exclaimed, "We shall never sleep tonight!"

Mark asked, "Shall we have a walk? It is still light and warm."

Luke said, "Carry on. I will answer the phone and explain that you are with your friends."

"Thank you."

Out they went.

Luke promised, "I will let the Contessa have the film and last night's interview."

Lady Teresa said she would ring Sophie. As Amanda's friends were with her, her aunt knew Lady Teresa would contact her before bed.

The team – Bob, Luke and Adam – came for breakfast. Whilst they were breakfasting, Julian came.

"Excuse me, ma'am, Reverend Brian is on the line for Chief Superintendent Young."

He gave the phone to Mark, who asked, "Excuse me?"

Brian said, "St David's are without a pianist for their 10 a.m. service. Mrs Moor, the pianist, has had a bad fall and their second pianist is away. I thought of you because you know the songs and hymns they sing at St David's.

Mark asked Amanda if she minded going to St David's rather than St James', and she asked everyone else. They said they didn't mind, but it would be a rush to get there for 10 a.m.

Mark told Brian, "We will get there as soon as possible, but it may be more like 10.15."

"They will be so relieved to have a pianist. Thank the Commander and the others. They have a lady vicar, Reverend Ryan."

Mark said, "You had better warn them that there will be thirteen of us, and the Commander will need to be at the front."

"Leave it with me. Thank you, Chief Superintendent."

Mark asked Amanda, "Can we go to six-o'clock evensong?"

Amanda looked round the table. "Yes please."

Mark told Brian.

After Mark had given Julian the phone, he said, "It would be nice if Robert met Adam as they are the same age."

Amanda asked Mark to ring the Reverend whilst they were on their way to the church.

They got a move on and arrived at St David's at 10.15. Robert was waiting for them. He was very happy. He, Mark, Luke and Adam went in first. Adam had his recorder. They introduced themselves to Reverend Ryan, Mrs Moor, Alan (the vicar's husband), and Terry (who helped with the computer).

Mark looked at the music and programme: "No problem," he said.

Amanda came in on her crutches. Everyone stood up as they

went to sit at the front. Joan and Stan made Amanda comfortable with her leg rest.

Reverend Ryan welcomed them and thanked them for coming; she also thanked Mark for playing for them. She told Amanda how thrilled they all were at her and her father's win for the charities. She had already announced the church notices, so they began with a song everyone knew. Reverend Ryan sat next to Amanda.

It was a very informal service, geared to include young children. During Reverend Ryan's sermon she had the children all in groups to illustrate what she had just said. They greatly enjoyed this and then one member from each group was asked to explain what they had done.

The Ashwood group added to the humour. Everyone was thrilled with them. The service finished at 11.15.

Mark introduced Mrs Moor to Amanda, who asked, "Have you any family?"

"Only my husband."

"Would you like to come back with us for lunch, and then a rest outside under the canopy?"

"I would love to, Commander. Thank you." She asked Alan to ring Graham and ask him to come down immediately.

Bob rang the local police station and asked, "Have you a patrol car going near Ashwood from St David's?"

They promised they would be there in a few minutes.

The dogs arrived, and the congregation went out to look at them.

Mark asked Amanda, "Can we come here next Sunday to help out?"

She said to the vicar, "With pleasure – we will do our best to get here for 10."

Reverend Ryan asked them not to rush, and she said if they were late, she would give the notices out and make any announcements.

Amanda told her, "We are taking Mr and Mrs Moor back as she is too unwell to cook. We will have a full house today, but I would like you and your family to come back with us next Sunday, if you can arrange it. We will take you and bring you home."

Reverend Ryan was over the moon.

Then Amanda noticed that Terry was standing by the piano, and she asked Mark to ask him if he was on his own. When he said he was, Amanda asked him if he wanted to come back with the young men.

"Thank you, Commander," he said as he rushed out.

They laughed.

Joan rang Mrs Burton to say there would be four extra guests for lunch.

"No problem," she said, "we expected this!"

There was right confusion outside. All the neighbours had come out to see the Commander and congratulate her on winning the quiz.

She said, "The audience enabled us to."

The police car came and Luke sorted everyone into the cars. Everybody waved goodbye, and said what a lovely morning it had been.

After eating a delicious lunch with great gusto, conversation flowed. Bob had to go home to prepare some work, and Amanda and Joan went upstairs. The team knew where the lounge was, and Robert took Terry and Mr Moor. Sandra made Mrs Moor comfortable in a chair outside with a cup of tea; and later her husband walked down to the river.

Amanda and Joan joined their guests. The team asked if they could go for a run round to view the countryside, and Mark arranged this with the dog handlers. Luke, Stan, Adam, Terry and Robert went to see the old cars. Mr Moor was very informative, pointing out places of interest to them. Everyone enjoyed it. They all met up for afternoon tea outside at the tables.

They went to the service at St James'. It was a lovely short service. Everyone congratulated the Commander on winning the quiz; she told them the audience had helped. They also thanked her for the interview, and said her words would greatly help people and set a good example.

Luke went home to prepare for work, and Adam went to study for his exam on the following Tuesday. He was returning to Cambridge from Ashwood after breakfast. Terry walked home from St James'. They dropped Mr and Mrs Moor off, and said they would see her next Sunday. The vicar, Reverend Ryan, had arranged to ring Mark at the end of the week with the hymns and songs.

The team decided to go swimming at the Morley, knowing the Commander had to go to her room after a busy day. Mark said he would fetch the dogs as per usual for their walk, but he didn't. They were restless outside Amanda's room – they knew the routine. Amanda thought Mark had gone swimming with the team; all three girls were beautiful and full of life.

Her parents thought Amanda was quiet, but knew she must be tired after all the excitement since Friday. When Amanda linked up with the Contessa, she also thought Amanda was quiet and a bit down, which was most unusual for her.

She asked, "Are you tired?"

Amanda said, "Mark hasn't fetched the dogs, so he must have gone swimming with the team." She said, "The girls are very beautiful and sports mad."

The Contessa said, "I will be disappointed if he has done so. He didn't appear to be like that."

Amanda was nearly crying.

Miss Biggin said, "Come on, Commander – bed. A good night's sleep is what you need." Then they heard the dogs barking excitedly and Miss Biggin said, "Here's Chief Superintendent Mark." (She nearly said 'Mark' – she was so pleased he had come.)

He stood in the doorway (he didn't come up after dinner).

Sophie said, "Stay linked, Amanda" – she wasn't going to miss this!

Mark had a great big bunch of sweet peas! He was perspiring and red in the face.

Amanda invited, "Come in. I thought you had gone swimming with my colleagues."

"I only go swimming with you, Amanda."

The Contessa asked Mark to speak to her.

He crouched down at the side of Amanda and showed her the sweet peas. "I have been to fetch them," he told the Contessa. "I overheard a man at the Spring Fair saying he grew them and had some almost ready. I arranged to fetch them today and this has been the only opportunity. I didn't say anything to Amanda. I wanted it to be a surprise. When I got there it wasn't a garden, as I had thought, but allotments! A crowd was waiting for me to ask me to pass their congratulations on to Amanda for the interview and the quiz. They are so proud that she has chosen to come here to get better. I was so frustrated to be delayed. I didn't want to be rude to them but I said I really must go.

Sophie told him, "You are a wonderful man. Amanda is very vulnerable just now."

"I know – I wouldn't let her and the dogs down deliberately."

The Contessa asked to speak to Amanda, who was sniffing the sweet peas! She told her, "You look more yourself now."

"Sorry."

Sophie promised, "I will ring you at 11 tomorrow morning, after your colleagues have left. I have a surprise for you." She told Amanda to give Mark a kiss from her.

Mark heard and said, "Well?"

She kissed him and fell asleep on his shoulder!

Sophie said to Mark, "Stay connected!"

Mark lifted Amanda, and Miss Biggin eased her robe off and straightened her nightie. He prayed they would both have an unbroken night's sleep.

Miss Biggin said, "Thank you. You are such a wonderful man, I could kiss you myself!"

Mark went back to the Contessa: "Lady Amanda is fast asleep."

She told him, "I have been concerned, but I know Amanda must be tired after the weekend; I have never known Amanda to be emotional and she certainly was never jealous of Andrew." She then said goodnight to him and Miss Biggin.

Mark switched off the computer and took the dogs for their walk after telling them he was sorry he was late. They appeared to understand. He couldn't believe Amanda had been jealous at the thought of him swimming with her team; he was filled with confidence and joy.

The Contessa rang Amanda's parents and told them of this incident. They were delighted, because they had such a high regard for Mark – having known him for four years, since Andrew's death. Amanda had never been jealous of Andrew. "Poor Mark – rushing to get back to her and being delayed!" They felt his frustration.

Sophie said, "I must go. I will ring Amanda in the morning at 11 with a surprise."

Lady Teresa asked what the surprise was.

She told her, "If I tell you, it will not be a surprise!"

They all laughed with a new happiness.

Next morning Amanda texted Mark: 'Darling Mark, I have slept all night without cramp. Isn't that wonderful? Your sweet peas are heavenly.'

Mark texted back: 'That's my girl. Be as quick as you can.'

She was.

Miss Biggin went down with the dogs to take them for a walk! She said, "The Commander is waiting. I will be back in about ten minutes."

Mark laughed and ran up the stairs. Amanda was sat on the settee. He rushed over, took her in his arms and they kissed passionately. He told her, "I adore you."

"I adore you."

He said, "I have to keep pinching myself – I think I have died and gone to Paradise!"

Amanda laughed. "Same here."

Mark asked her, "Do you love me enough to marry me?"

She told him, "I certainly do. Wait until the team have gone back and we will be able to talk then."

Miss Biggin came back whistling!

Luke, Adam and the team came to breakfast. Everyone knew there was something happening with Amanda and Mark. Electricity surrounded them.

Amanda told them, "I have slept through the night without cramps."

They were all thrilled and promised to keep praying.

Amanda thanked them.

Peter asked, "What are you doing this morning, ma'am?"

She told them, "I am having my swimming therapy with Chief Superintendent Mark. My aunt, the Contessa, has told me she will ring me at 11 this morning with a surprise."

Adam asked, "What is it, Commander?"

"If I knew, it wouldn't be a surprise."

They all laughed.

Adam said, "Sorry."

"I am intrigued," Amanda told them.

Sharon asked, "Does the Contessa sing?"

"No," replied Amanda, "she isn't musical, but she adores the opera and good music." She went on: "I think it is more likely she, somehow, despite her heart condition, has found a way to come to this area to be near me. I pray I am right. I adore her. Chief Superintendent Mark set up the computer camera link. It is spot-on. He bought me a big bunch of sweet peas last night, and I showed her – isn't that wonderful?"

Helen asked, "You like sweet peas, Commander?"

"I love them," she replied. "I always have. The colours – the perfume is like no other."

Stephen thanked her for the weekend. "It has been a great eye-opener. Please excuse me for saying this – we are all thinking it –we have discovered you are human. Who would have thought you loved sweet peas? As our commander, you are first class, ma'am, but remote – though we have always been able to come to you with our work problems. We appreciate how you have helped us, and we understand that in your position you have needed to stay focused."

"Yes," agreed Amanda, "that's the problem." She went on: "It was difficult for me when I knew you were coming. I welcomed this, but wondered what was going to happen."

They laughed.

"Then I saw you – I melted. It was on that wonderful Saturday afternoon when you preferred the cars to swimming with me – you made the decision without bowing to me. It's given me an insight into our chief. He is a friend of my parents – plays golf with my dada, and comes to our home for dinner. I have always disappeared when he has visited – our relationship is professional. It has to be in our job."

Helen said, "He is very dishy, ma'am."

"I suppose he is."

"He always looks immaculate," Sharon acknowledged. "We are surprised he isn't married. He admires you, Commander."

Amanda laughed. "Good gracious, the Derbyshire air must have gone to your brain! Thank goodness our relationship has been remote! However would I have coped with you?"

They all laughed.

Cheryl said, "We have had a wonderful weekend and we can't thank you enough, Commander."

Amanda said, "The pleasure has been all mine."

Then Stan and Adam took them to the railway station. Adam's train to Cambridge was also due in. Luke had set off for Germany and the football. Amanda, Joan and Mark had a glass of beer while they waited for the Contessa's call.

Chapter 9

At 11 a.m. the Contessa rang, enquiring if Amanda's colleagues had left.

Amanda said, "Yes, Aunt. It has been a wonderful God-blessed weekend."

Then the Contessa told her the surprise: "Lord and Lady Hayward from Chiverton Manor, three miles from Ashwood, visited your Aunt Cynthia and me on Saturday. They are hoping to buy a property near the villa to live in. They love Italy and the operas. Their son, Matthew, a rising solicitor (Amanda's dada knew him), and his wife will continue to live in London to further his career. They like the lifestyle there. They want to buy a larger home to start a family, so Chiverton Manor is to be sold."

Amanda listened in silence. "There are twenty bedrooms, most of them en-suite." Her aunt went on: "I want to buy it for you, darling. It is a wonderful opportunity. You like the area – it will be useful for weekends, or whatever, darling. [She knew, after the sweet peas episode the night before, that Mark and Amanda were in love.] View it first, Amanda. May the local solicitor, Mr Lucas, come for lunch to discuss it?"

Amanda answered in her forthright way, "This is overwhelming, dearest darling. It sounds fine with me. I accept if it is suitable – and of course Mr Lucas will be very welcome."

Her aunt went on: "If you do not like it, something else will turn up. I will ring off now so you can discuss this with darling Mark and Joan."

Amanda excused herself and rang Mrs Burton to say, "One more for lunch, please."

She asked Mark to invite his dad. She then told Mark and Joan about Chiverton. Stan came hurrying back. She told him about Chiverton Manor and went into the full details the Contessa had given her. She suggested they had a coffee each.

Joan and Stan said they would leave her and Mark on their own –they knew they were in love.

Amanda told Mark, "If we do not like it, or it is unsuitable, there will be somewhere else."

Mark gulped. "You really are going to marry me?"

She replied, laughing, "Of course I am, you fool!"

He said, "That's all right, then" – one of Amanda's favourite sayings. Then they kissed. "We'll talk later."

Amanda teased him with "I have something better for your lips to do!"

He laughed with great joy. He couldn't believe it.

Jack Lucas arrived early. He told Amanda, "This is a wonderful opportunity – a beautiful home, forty years old, 200 acres, a wood, lake, river. A spring provides water through a pumping system. A few gypsies live in the wood – they have for as long as anyone could remember. They are security for the Manor, and they keep the rabbits down."

They were all dumbstruck.

Then Amanda asked, "Have you brought photographs?"

"No," he replied. "The Contessa wants you to see it first-hand. May I instruct one of my team to film the rooms? With the greatest respect, ma'am, a film will enable you to view the Manor on a screen here. Are you free to visit this afternoon, ma'am?"

Amanda looked round the table and everyone said they were free. They were all filled with joy.

Amanda said, "We must take Bob if he is free."

Mark rang him, and asked him if he could be at Chiverton for 2.30. "Amanda wants to take you out for afternoon tea," he said.

"Try and keep me away," Bob replied. "Where are we going?"

Mark laughed. "It's a surprise."

Bob worked through his lunch hour.

Amanda suggested that Mrs Burton might also want to come with them.

She accepted with pleasure, though Amanda did not tell her exactly where they were going.

Mr Lucas asked, "May I ring Mrs Ashby, the housekeeper? Lady Hayward has told her in confidence that they are selling, and that I will be bringing a prospective buyer this afternoon."

When he told Mrs Ashby the news, he asked, "Are you able to provide afternoon tea for seven?"

Mrs Ashby said, "Of course. I have a reliable woman I can call on to help me."

At 12.30 they had lunch. When they had been served, Mr Lucas informed Amanda, "There are 250 houses in the village belonging to the Manor – also eleven farms spread out. Mrs Ashby is now sixty-five years old, and her husband is seventy. They live in the caretaker's bungalow inside the gates. Their daughter, in her thirties, is expecting her first child; she and her husband live in one of the 250 houses. Mr and Mrs Ashby are retiring to a council bungalow in the village. They want to help their daughter and enjoy their first grandchild and their retirement."

Amanda agreed: "Of course – after they have worked all their lives!"

"Also, ma'am, the manager, who is in charge of collecting rent from the houses and farms, is looking at retirement – he is sixty-eight years old."

Amanda said, "It will be a new start for whoever buys the Manor."

Mr Lucas went on: "It is a beautiful building. An intensive survey was undertaken last week for any damage, and there is no problem. The staff have made sure it has been kept in good repair. There are stables at the back of the house, a flower garden and greenhouse." He then said he had better not say any more, but they all could tell he thought it was wonderful.

Amanda and Joan went upstairs. Amanda asked Joan, "If I do have the Manor, will you live with me?" She went on: "You know, Mark and I are in love and we will marry."

Joan burst out crying with happiness, hugging Amanda and saying, "Good girl! Darling, I will be honoured to live with you and be around when the babies come."

Amanda laughed. "Give me a chance to marry first!" Amanda asked her, "Should I ask Stan to live with us? It sounds big enough for you both to have your own suite of rooms."

Joan said, "He will love that. He is such a good man, like Mark and his brothers."

"They are, aren't they, Joan? How can Isabel have left them?"

Bob arrived at 2.15. Amanda and Joan were still upstairs. He was curious when he saw the car, the dogs, and the chair being put in. It was a most beautiful warm afternoon. Amanda came down and, after greeting him with a kiss, told him, "We are going to view Chiverton Manor, Bob. Do you know it?"

He replied, "Wow! It is a beauty. Are we ready?"

Mrs Burton came carrying a tin with a fruit cake in it! Mr Lucas followed them.

As they were going through the gates, Amanda asked Ben to pull up. They gazed at the Manor in the near distance. It was built in beautiful golden Cotswold stone – youthful but quality. It had wonderful windows, so clean-looking and well cared for. They went on and found Mr and Mrs Ashby outside waiting for them. A corgi was chasing around. When Amanda was in her chair, Mrs Ashby curtsied and welcomed her. Amanda felt at home before she had even entered the house.

Cambridge and Oxford and Amanda's dogs ran to play with the corgi, and were soon the best of friends. Ben knew this visit was in confidence.

Mr Lucas informed her, "The photographer is getting on well, ma'am."

Amanda thanked him. "Good."

They went into the hall. It had a wonderful, spacious marble floor, with long settees on each side. Two tables were decorated with wonderful flower arrangements. All the wood was 100% solid with a pale, golden-grained pattern. A giant chandelier hung in the centre.

Bob said, "Let's leave them on their own for a while."

They were in awe, both crying. Mark crouched down and they cuddled and kissed. They kept saying they couldn't believe it.

Mark said, "It is wonderful, and this is just the hall!"

The dogs lay down as though they felt they had come home. Mr Lucas came back then showed Amanda a hidden elevator. The Contessa had told him to keep that as a surprise. Mr Lucas said the Commander would not need it soon, but it was useful for carrying things up stairs or down. Amanda agreed.

Amanda asked to see the kitchen. They went past a very big dining room, with a huge marble open fire, into a large room with a big scrubbed table, a huge Welsh dresser full of pots, a long sideboard, two rocking chairs and another big marble fireplace.

Amanda exclaimed, "What a wonderful breakfast room!"

They went on into the kitchen – a huge country kitchen! – with another huge scrubbed table, a Welsh dresser, an enormous Aga and a twelve-ring gas cooker! Beside another big log fireplace, herbs, garlic, onions and cooking pots hung from the ceiling.

Everywhere was beautiful, clean, light and airy.

Amanda asked Mrs Ashby where the six doors led. On one side three doors led to a scullery for preserving fruits, etc. and a flower-arranging area; to a wine cellar; and to a shower/bath area for the dogs. The opposite three led to a sewing room; to a sitting room with a table, chairs, settees, a TV and another log fire; and to a utility room for leaving boots and hanging coats, with a separate toilet. As well as the fireplaces, all the rooms had central heating provided by a separate oil unit in the Aga. Mark was very interested in that.

Mrs Ashby asked, "May I put out the afternoon tea, ma'am?"

"Yes please," said Amanda, "on the outside table."

Mrs Burton and Joan helped her.

They went out into the garden, and Mr Ashby came with them. Cows and sheep were grazing at the back behind a wire fence. There was a stream running down the field.

Amanda said, "We will be able to grow watercress."

Everybody laughed.

There was no doubt Amanda was going to accept the Contessa's offer.

Mr Ashby told them, "There is a marvellous compost heap at the end of the garden. It has been rotting down for years. The gardener makes liquid fertiliser from it using water from a rainwater cistern. Mark was very interested in this (he was thinking he would be able to grow sweet peas for Amanda).

They noticed the gypsies in the distance, looking at them from the wood. They all waved, and the gypsies waved back.

Mr Ashby said, "They are afraid the new owners may move them. They are no trouble – in fact, they are a blessing. They look after the wood and keep the rabbits down."

Bob said there had never been any trouble from them.

Amanda said, "Good! they can stay, but I will ask them to remove any traps from the wood, where the dogs will be running."

Mr Ashby suggested the gypsies could fence off the copse, and put their traps there.

Amanda said, "Good idea!"

"Mrs Shulot cleans the kitchens every morning and other times when needed," he said. "She is a wonderful worker, spotlessly clean."

"I'm pleased," said Amanda. "Is she willing to carry on?"

"Yes. She will be grateful and so will the other workers."

Joan and Mark took Amanda up in the elevator – Joan had brought the equipment! Mark looked round as he waited for them.

Amanda said, "This is wonderful. I can't wait to see the film!"

Mr Lucas arranged, with Amanda's permission, for a screen to be put up in her sitting room. The film was ready for after breakfast the next day.

Before they went down, Amanda asked Mark, "Would your dad like to live here with us? Joan is coming."

Mark couldn't stop the tears. He said, "Thank you, thank you, Amanda darling. Yes please."

When Amanda asked Stan, he also cried with thankfulness.

They returned for afternoon tea, and sat and gazed down to the lake. They could see the swans, ducks, and colourful birds, and then, below, the river running across at the bottom.

Bob teased Amanda: "You are worth quite a bit now, aren't you?"

"Yes," she laughed. "Would you like to marry me?"

They all laughed.

They all tucked into the lovely sandwiches, scones, fruit cake and cheese. Amanda texted the Contessa (it was her rest time): 'Thank you, darling. So far, so good. Confirm tomorrow but take it as read.'

Amanda asked Bob, "Can you come tomorrow morning to view the film with us?"

He laughingly said, "I had better put in for some holidays. Yes please! I will do some work this evening; this should leave me free for a couple of hours tomorrow."

Ben came and they went back to Ashwood. Mrs Burton had arranged dinner for half an hour later, so Amanda and Mark had time for their swim. Joan let Miss Biggin know.

Before Miss Biggin came, Amanda rang Dougie on his secure line to tell him about Chiverton – she had promised to tell him any news first. She said, "If you like, you can broadcast Wednesday evening, saying the Contessa has offered to buy it for me." She promised to fax him more information and photographs.

He was very grateful – he needed something good.

When Miss Biggin and Amanda were upstairs, she told her about Chiverton. She was overjoyed.

Amanda asked her, "Can you stay tomorrow, have breakfast, then watch the film with us?"

Miss Biggin said, "Yes please." She said, "I feel a fraud being called a night nurse now that you are sleeping through without cramps."

Amanda told her, "I still need you if I have to go to the loo during the night."

Miss Biggin laughed and said, "Yes."

Amanda spoke to Contessa Sophie via the camera link: "You have made me so happy, Aunt. Thank you. I love Chiverton – it is marvellous."

Sophie knew she had stayed often with Lord and Lady Hayward. She said, "Lady Hayward says we can buy any furniture, carpets or paintings you want."

Amanda asked her aunt, "May I have the hand-painted piano from the villa and the large portrait of you from the sitting room?"

The Contessa said, "They will be shipped over – also my collection of crystal glasses, etc. [These were priceless.] Anything else?" asked Sophie.

"I will let you know, thank you, darling."

Sophie laughed. Amanda was so like her – forthright. She told Amanda, "I have always adored you, and you have always made me happy and given me something to live for. Now I have seen you and Mark are so in love, I will die happy."

Amanda begged her not to die.

The Contessa laughingly said, "I will do my best, if only to see your first baby."

"I pray" Amanda promised her, "we will have at least one."

Her aunt asked, "Whilst we are sending a shipment, would you like the Lamborghini? When you start with your babies you will want to stay at Chiverton."

"Yes," agreed Amanda, "that will be sensible until they are older."

She next rang her parents, to tell them how wonderful Chiverton is. They also had visited Lord and Lady Hayward a few years before.

"The sale is going through," her dada said. "We are so happy for you and Mark."

The film showed an absolutely beautiful home. Sixteen of the bedrooms were en-suite; a wide corridor upstairs ran the width of the house; the windows ensured plenty of light; the views were spectacular. The master bedroom was huge with a big, wonderful fireplace. The bathroom was all marble – glorious. There was a dressing room, and a large, empty room with another wonderful fireplace. Amanda, seeing this, thought of having a large cast-iron bath installed so she and Mark could relax in it and talk. She kept this to herself. Every bedroom had central heating. From the window balcony they could see the lake nearby with ducks and other wildlife, and the river running across the bottom of the lawn.

The bedrooms on both sides had balconies. Amanda suggested Stan and Joan had these rooms.

"Yes please. I will be able to sketch and paint."

Joan said she would be able to sit outside to knit and embroider.

Amanda asked them to sort out which side they would like; Mark chose his temporary rooms, and Luke and Adam chose their rooms. Downstairs were a very large music room, a large sitting room, and several smaller rooms. It was all wonderful – so clean and light. At the back was an enclosed swimming pool. Amanda suggested they made the room next to it into a gymnasium.

They returned to Chiverton after lunch, and went to see Mr and Mrs Shulot and family. The men bowed to her and Mrs Shulot curtsied.

Amanda asked them, "Please remove all the traps from the wood – my dogs will be running free. I will have the copse fenced off and you can put your traps in there."

They thanked her. "We are so grateful you are allowing us to stay, Lady Amanda."

Amanda admired their dogs – three German shepherds and one Jack Russell. She asked Mrs Shulot, "Are you willing to stay on at Chiverton?"

She said, "Oh, yes please, ma'am."

Mr Shulot asked, "Have you any more dogs, Commander?"

She told him, "I have a Rottweiler, Thunder. My dada bought it for me when I used to gallop on Sussex Downs. I have never been in any fear. My horse is such a big, powerful animal that sometimes it took all my strength to hold him."

"You must be missing them."

"Yes, but when the sale has gone through, and everything is in order, I will have them brought up."

Mrs Shulot asked, "Will you be living here, Lady Amanda?"

"When I go back to the Met, working part-time until my leg is stronger, I will come here for long weekends."

They were very pleased and promised they would do anything for her.

Mr Shulot said, "If you bring the old cars here, ma'am, everything will be safe. Our dogs are aware of anyone from three miles off."

Amanda laughed. She asked, "Who owns the cows and sheep?"

They said, "Chiverton, ma'am."

"And the horses?"

"They are my sons'. We will move them, Lady Amanda."

"I cannot see any problem. What happens to them during the winter?"

"A friend stables them. If your horse is too strong for you, when your knee is better, Lady Amanda, you could perhaps ride one of these horses."

"Perhaps," she replied.

"My eldest son wondered if you would like a small trap with one of the horses to pull it, ma'am?"

"That is something for me to think about – it is a good idea, thank you."

Mrs Shulot said, "Ma'am, please do not think we will interfere with you. We know what is correct, Commander."

Amanda said, "I am sure you do."

"Ma'am, we are so honoured you are coming here."

"It is all in confidence just now." Amanda laughed.

Mr Shulot said, "With all reverence, ma'am, in this community not much goes unnoticed."

They all laughed.

He asked, "Do you like rabbit?"

"Yes we do. Fresh is wonderful."

He fetched six plump rabbits. "No shot in these, ma'am!" he said as he put them in a bag with a tray of mushrooms collected that morning.

Mark took them. "Thank you. We will enjoy these. Bye for now."

As they were moving away they heard Mr Shulot saying, "I have never seen anyone so beautiful, Ella, and she is a proper lady."

They went back to the house for afternoon tea, staying outside in the beautiful sunshine again.

Mrs Burton was thrilled with the rabbits and mushrooms. "Better than ours here!" she said.

The sale went through. Sophie was a billionaire thanks to her business dealings in stocks and shares, including her one-third share in London Masons, plus property she owned in London and Italy. She released enough money for Amanda to make any improvements and buy new furniture, carpets, etc. Lord and Lady Dansie released money from a trust fund they had set up when Amanda was born; also they released the same amount for Joshua and his family from his trust fund.

On Wednesday afternoon they repeated the pattern. Whilst they were having afternoon tea Mrs Burton asked Amanda, "May I have a word, ma'am?"

"Is it private?"

"No," she replied, "we are all friends."

Mrs Burton asked, "Will you consider me for the post of housekeeper at Chiverton?"

Amanda was surprised. "What about Ashwood, Mrs Burton?"

"As you know, ma'am, Lady Cynthia will be retiring as mistress of Ashwood soon and Lord Richard will be returning with his new bride. I am due to retire in six years and I would be more comfortable with you." Mrs Burton went on: "I really am not up to all the new plans they have."

Amanda said, "You will be very welcome. When will you be leaving?"

"When will you need me, ma'am?"

"Right, leave this with me," answered Amanda; "and thank you, I am reassured to know you will be running the household."

"Thank you, ma'am. Also, ma'am, there are others who want to come."

Amanda said laughingly, "This is supposed to be confidential!"

Mrs Burton admitted, "I am sorry but in this district nothing is secret."

Bob agreed.

Amanda then said, "I have asked Sandra and Julian. They are coming."

Mrs Burton knew – they had told her!

Amanda then asked, "What ever will my cousin, Lord Richard, say?"

Bob then asked Amanda, "May I have a word?"

"Of course. Are you applying for the post of housekeeper?"

He laughed. "No. My sister and brother-in-law are retiring to Cornwall: I wondered if it is possible for me to buy or rent the caretaker's bungalow at the gates. My home will be too big for me when they have left. If you agree, Commander, I can employ a daily to look after me. I would be able to meet up with Stan, Joan and friends in my free evenings, when I do not have to work or prepare."

Amanda said, "That sounds all right with me."

Mark said, "That will be brilliant. Amanda will like you to be near her."

Amanda then asked, "Is it big enough?"

"Yes, there will be only me sleeping there."

Amanda then asked, "Would you like an extension?"

He answered, "I wouldn't mind a conservatory so I could see the views."

"Right," said Amanda, "choose a design and we will have it

built with the proper foundations; but you are very welcome to live in the house with us, Bob."

"Thank you, Amanda," he said, "but the bungalow will suit me perfectly."

"Good! You will understand that I prefer you to rent, not buy."

"Whatever you say, Amanda. Thank you and God bless you."

Amanda then said, "Things are taking shape very satisfactorily."

Stan asked, "I also would like a word, Amanda."

They all laughed.

"Yes?"

"As you know, I am retiring next week and I wonder if I may apply to be manager in charge of the rent collecting? I am positive my three car friends would like to come with me to collect the rents. It would be a social thing."

"When is the present manager retiring?"

"At the end of this month. I could ask him to show me the routine and bookwork before he leaves."

Amanda looked at Mark. "Thank you, Uncle Stan. That sounds just fine to me, but I do not want you to be burdened. I want you to enjoy your retirement and have time to renovate the old cars, sketch and paint. You are very precious to me. Let's make an appointment with the manager to find out what the job entails. Perhaps it will take up enough of your time collecting the farm rents with your friends?"

Mark was nodding.

Stan told her, "We all want to help you."

"Thank you, darling. I know."

Joan asked, "I would like to visit the farms sometimes when you do not need me."

Stan told her, "My friends and I will welcome you. The farmers give vegetables and new-laid eggs!"

Amanda then said, "Talking about eggs, we could have hens, couldn't we?"

They all said, "Yes."

"I will ask Mr Lucas about the cows and sheep in the field. Mr Shulot says they belong to Chiverton. Also, I have two remaining cows and six sheep at Ashwood."

They laughed. "We didn't know that."

"The beef and lamb we have been eating are from my animals.

The two cows and the sheep can be moved down to us."

Dougie announced in his programme, "Contessa Sophie has bought Chiverton Manor in Derbyshire, three miles from Ashwood, for her heiress, Commander Amanda Dansie. He showed photographs. "The Commander will use it for weekends whilst working part-time for the Met when her knee is sorted." The newspapers and other television and radio programmes also carried the story.

Amanda had many requests to be interviewed. She asked Dougie to let other reporters know there was nothing to add to his interview with her – apart from Chiverton Manor, which she was thrilled about. She said she would reconsider when she felt stronger, but for now her time would be spent looking after Chiverton Manor, and undergoing physical therapies to get her leg healed. She said she hoped they understood.

Chapter 10

A few days later, after she had spoken to the Contessa, she asked to speak to Lady Cynthia. She told her, "The Commissioner wants to come with my parents for lunch on the 20th May. Is this OK, Aunt?"

Lady Cynthia said, "You do not have to ask me anything, Amanda. You know you can do what you want – you are paying! Ashwood and everyone are so thrilled when your guests come; they have never had so much excitement in their lives!"

Amanda laughed and thanked her.

She rang Mrs Burton. "I need to see you when convenient, please. My boss, the Commissioner, wants to come with my parents for lunch on Friday 20th May. May I invite some senior police and whoever the Commissioner would like to meet?"

Mrs Burton said, "I am very honoured – and, ma'am, you do not have to ask me."

The chefs at the Morley were over the moon, and they began to make preparations for this day. Marcos, Lady Teresa's Italian chef, and his lady assistant, came to help cook the Italian food, and they welcomed this. Because it was such an honour to cook for the Met chief, they wanted it to be perfect.

Amanda reassured them: "Everything you do is perfect – you two are equal to any."

They were filled with confidence by her words. They thanked her and promised to get their suggested menus to her as soon as possible after they had sorted out what local produce would be available. They thanked her for giving them space to organise this.

Amanda went on: "Marcos will serve the wines – he is trained at that." She then asked to see Julian and when he was free she said to him, "Can you and your group arrange a rock-and-roll time for the 20th of May, when the Commissioner, my parents and other guests are coming?"

He said, "With pleasure, ma'am. We have the music ready – we have been looking forward to this." (The Commissioner's PA had previously given Amanda the rock-and-roll music he liked.)

She then rang her chief and suggested he travel up with her parents, Dougie and a cameraman.

He said, "We will come in the helicopter – and thank you."

"Do you like Italian, sir?"

"I love it, ma'am."

"I will fax the menus, sir, to your PA. May I invite some senior police who would like to meet you?"

"That will suit me very well, thank you, Commander."

"Please let me know, sir, if there is anyone else you would like to meet."

"Thank you, ma'am. I will do that – speak to you soon."

Amanda rang her mum back.

"The chefs welcome Marcos and his assistant coming. I have booked them into the Morley. Please let me have his suggested menus as soon as possible."

Lady Teresa assured her, "I will attend to this at once. Let me know if I can help you further. Your dada is sending up plenty of wines."

She told her mum, "I do thank you, Mum, for everything – also Dada. This lunch will be quite unnerving for me."

"You will be wonderful, darling. Just be yourself and enjoy it."

Amanda then rang Dougie on his secure line.

"Dougie, are you free to come for lunch on Friday the 20th? My boss, the Commissioner, and my parents are coming up for lunch and a musical afternoon. My chief suggested you and your cameraman travel with them in the helicopter."

Dougie said, "I am delighted. Thank you for this. I will take this opportunity to ask the Commissioner and your dada to give me an interview."

Amanda laughed. "Go for it, Dougie."

He asked, "Is this just a social happening or something special?"

Amanda told him, "I promised to always let you be the first to know – I am giving the Commissioner my resignation."

"I thought that. And are you announcing your engagement to Chief Superintendent Mark at the same time?"

"No," she laughed. "That will be later. You will be told! Be in touch. I will fax the menus. My mum's Italian chef is coming up to help."

Dougie said, "I am looking forward to this immensely. Will I be allowed to use clips in my programme?"

"Of course. I trust you. Bye for now."

When Amanda and Joan went down they met up with Mark, and Amanda told him the progress she had made so far. "Now we have to plan who should be invited from among the senior police."

Mark made some suggestions and said, "When Bob comes he will help."

Bob did.

Amanda told him, "I am giving the Commissioner my resignation, Bob. My dada, being a close friend, is going to prepare him before he comes, but we need to keep this confidential between us."

Bob teased: "They will guess!"

Mark, Amanda and Joan sent off the invitations on Adam's illustrated cards, which said there would be a musical time in the afternoon, and requested, 'Please let us know if you want to take part. We have a rock-and-roll group – this is especially for the Commissioner!'

Wednesday, Thursday and Friday were a hive of activity! Everyone was so excited by this honour. The local photographers and newsreel were invited to meet the Commissioner after lunch. Bob put discreet extra security on.

Just before 12 p.m. the helicopter arrived. Mark went to meet it. Amanda was in her chair in order to be mobile.

The Commissioner said, "What a beautiful sight!"

She laughed.

His bodyguard and Dougie greeted her. Her dada and mum cuddled her. Bob, Stan and Julian took the men to the pool lounge. They left their jackets – it was so hot. Mark took the Commissioner up to his room. Sandra attended to the ladies. When they returned, the Judge asked to excuse them, and the Commissioner, Amanda and Mark went into a private room. Lady Teresa was being the hostess until Amanda returned. Everyone introduced themselves. The waiters brought drinks.

The Commissioner said to Amanda, "Commander, your dada has informed me that you are deeply in love with Chief Superintendent Young, and you tell me your aunt, the Contessa, has bought you Chiverton Manor?"

"Yes, sir, that is correct."

He went on: "My only concern is that Chief Superintendent Young was your fiancé's colonel, and, with the shock of your leg wound and the loss of members of your team, and the transition from being super-active to more or less being on holiday here, your emotions may be topsy-turvy. Perhaps you are escaping from reality."

Everyone went quiet. Mark's hands were clenched, but he dare not say anything.

Amanda was angry – this was her moment. She said, "Thank you, sir. I appreciate you have my best interests at heart."

The Commissioner realised she was being sarcastic, and as he didn't want to lose her and all her expertise as Commander he laughed.

"But, sir, let me assure you that I am very deeply in love with Mark, and he returns my feelings. I am going to be his wife and, I pray, the mother of his children. We will live at Chiverton and I will be active in this community. So, sir, I offer you my resignation as your commander. I thank you for your help, advice and your confidence in me."

He said, "Very reluctantly I accept your resignation. I wish you and Chief Superintendent Young the greatest happiness in your new life."

He shook their hands, and then they went back to the other guests.

Julian came and said, "Lunch is served, ma'am."

Mark and Joan helped Amanda out of her chair onto her crutches, and she and Mark led them in.

Everywhere looked magnificent – a few ladies from the WI had arranged beautiful flowers, and the Contessa had sent silver and the crystal; the staff had indeed pulled all the stops out. Luke had previously photographed and filmed all this. The Commissioner was on Amanda's left, Mark on her right. Everyone gave their names and said what they did. Matthew said grace. They tucked into the wonderful food, and the Commissioner remarked on the quality.

Amanda said, "This is the freshest Ashwood produce, and the chefs here at the Morley are equal to any."

They all remarked on the wines.

Amanda told them, "My dada provided the wines."

The atmosphere was relaxed, with no awkward silences.

When the meal came to an end, the Commissioner toasted Amanda and said she was the perfect hostess – everyone had been included and conversation had flowed. (He had asked Amanda about Chiverton and her therapy.)

Her dada toasted Amanda and said, "Your mum and I are so proud of you. This is only the second time you have been hostess to a large gathering."

Everybody clapped.

When coffee had been served, and everyone was relaxing, the Commissioner went on to say, "I wish I was younger. Perhaps I would have stood a chance with the Commander." He went on, "Our relationship has been strictly professional – this is the first meal I have shared with her. Her parents often invite me for dinner, but she is always absent. However, one early evening after we had finished the day's work, we were discussing the next step in a very complex case. The Commander is very beautiful even in uniform and I thought I would chance it with her."

Amanda had her head bowed as she listened.

"I gave her a peck and she threw me right across the room with one of her SAS tricks. I lay there stunned – I have never been so embarrassed in my life. How did I get out of this with dignity? The Commander said, 'Right, shall we get on?'"

Amanda was bright red. She peeped at Mark, and saw that he was laughing. The Commissioner and everybody were laughing too.

Dougie said, "I can't use this story, but what a scoop it would be!"

Everyone laughed again.

Amanda asked if the chefs could spare time to come and be

thanked. Everyone clapped them and said, "Well done!"

Then Brian closed with a prayer of thankfulness.

Amanda apologised that there weren't more rest rooms available as the workmen were in.

They all went to freshen up for the photographs and newsreel films. Reporters had come to take photographs and local newsreels of the Commissioner from the Met. Everyone went outside. Dougie's cameraman switched on his links to ITV and the BBC ready to send.

The Commissioner began with, "I thank the Commander for inviting me, and I thank you for coming. What a wonderful lunch we have all enjoyed! The quality of the food was outstanding. I compliment the chefs. I am very pleased to be here. I haven't been before to this area, but hopefully I will come again soon. I have had the opportunity of talking with the police round the table and I hope to converse further with them. We at the Met want you to know how much we appreciate your help, support and advice. We work very well as a team. We all rely on one another. The Commander and I are from the Met, but we are no different to any of you. We are all doing our best to keep everyone safe and encouraging especially the young to lead good, wholesome lives. It isn't easy being in the force. We have the example of the Commander with her shattered knee. Members of her team were killed. But we have to have courage, and trust in God to help us. We live in an evil world – but there are good people everywhere, and good will overcome evil. Now it is with regret that I announce the resignation of Commander Amanda Dansie. The Met and I are very sorry to lose her. Her intelligence, perception, courage, dedication, leadership – everything she does – is 100%. Whilst she has been here she has continued to help me to solve two cases we have been working on. I wish her, on the Met's behalf, every happiness in her future life."

Dougie's cameraman sent off the film to ITV and the BBC. He mentioned that Amanda's resignation and parts of the musical afternoon would be shown on his evening programme!

They all went to freshen up and met in the music room. Lord Dansie played the violin accompanied by Amanda on the piano. Lady Teresa was silently crying.

When they had finished, Amanda quietly told her dada, "I will always be your little girl."

Next Amanda sang and then she and Mark performed a duet. The programme went through smoothly, and everyone was thrilled.

After the break, Amanda announced, "Especially for the Commissioner, there is now a rock-and-roll time!"

It certainly was wonderful. Everyone danced. The Commissioner loved it and thanked everyone.

He asked, "Has it been filmed?"

Luke said, "Yes, sir. I will have a copy ready for you before you leave."

Amanda's resignation was widely broadcast and excerpts of the afternoon's entertainment were shown. Flowers, letters and cards poured in as the news became known.

A week later Lord and Lady Dansie put an announcement in the newspaper: 'Our beloved only daughter, Amanda, and Chief Superintendent Young are getting engaged in July. Their marriage will take place in September. They will live at Chiverton Manor, Derbyshire. Further details will be later shared.'

The decorators moved into Chiverton, and new carpets and furniture from local shops were installed in the rooms that were, for the time being, going to be used. The special equipment Amanda still needed was installed in her bathroom and the downstairs loo. The cast-iron bath was installed in the room next to the master suite – the floor had to be reinforced. They and the dogs moved in and were all very happy. Tarquin and Thunder were brought up and they settled immediately. Amanda's car and helicopter came later. Amanda hired a battery-operated wheelchair, and she was even able to use it to go into the wood. She had had a road built. This would also be useful for the children to ride their bikes, etc.

Stan suggested he sell The Laurels, their home, and share the money with Mark, Luke, and Adam.

Amanda asked, "Will Isabel claim half?"

"Yes," said Stan.

"That doesn't matter," Amanda told him. "We are a family – what is mine is Mark's. Are you all happy here?"

Stan and Luke replied, "We certainly are, Amanda. We have never been so happy."

"Good! You are a great help to me and you will be even more useful when the babies start coming."

They all laughed.

Luke told them the small local fitness studio was up for sale, and he said he thought he might buy it with his share of the money. He wouldn't give up his job with the police but could work there on Saturdays. The manager was full of integrity, and Luke thought he might be persuaded to stay on.

Mark said, "We had better get Adam up to discuss selling The Laurels."

Adam said he didn't want to live there again now his mum had left.

The house was sold quickly for more than the price asked. Adam's share was put into a trust fund. Mark suggested to Amanda that with part of his share they could have an outdoor pool with a big block of toilets/showers; she welcomed this.

Stan received a real shock in a letter from Isabel:

'I apologise for leaving you and my three boys. Do you think you could forgive me for what I did and make a fresh start? You have now retired and with our money from our home we can have the holidays and cruises you had planned. We could also both live at Chiverton Manor. I look forward to hearing from you very soon.'

Stan showed Mark the letter. He was very concerned. "What do you want to do, Dad?"

"I do not trust her now, Mark. I have a fulfilled life here – but am I being selfish?"

"No," he said firmly "you are not. It's Mum who is selfish; she didn't think about any of us when she was planning to leave us. I may be wrong, but possibly it is my marrying Amanda, and our life here, which is attracting her. I'm sorry, Dad, but there is no way she can come here."

"Oh no, Mark, I know that."

"Do you still love her and want to be with her, Dad? Please tell me the truth."

"She was my wife, Mark, and we had you three; I thank her

for that, but no, it is better to remain apart now and I think have a quiet divorce."

He and Mark had a cry.

"We need to discuss this with Luke and Adam, Dad."

"Yes, of course, Mark."

When Amanda and Joan met with them for breakfast they knew something had upset both of them; they could see they had been crying.

Please do not think I am prying, but I can see you are both upset; do you want to talk about it?" she gently queried.

Mark told her.

She knew this was a real problerm, but between them she knew they would sort it out in the best way.

"It is a mess," admitted Mark.

"Yes," agreed Amanda. "Any long-standing relationship which breaks up is a mess. There is always fault on both side – that's human nature – but Isabel did leave you all when Stan was looking forward to spending time with her in his retirement."

They were all silent. Amanda was silently thinking, 'Isabel doesn't know me. I am not having her upsetting my new family.'

"Come on," she said. "You are all going to have a good breakfast. Just remember you have Joan and me now. We will not stand any nonsense from Isabel."

Because of her positive attitude, they all felt stronger. They recognised again her excellent qualities and understood why she had been made a commander at such a young age.

Mark rang Adam's tutor and explained the situation. He asked if Adam could come to Chiverton for the weekend.

The tutor was very sympathetic and said, "Of course. Adam will be able to come on Saturday morning and return for Monday morning. If I can help you further, sir, please keep me informed."

Mark thanked him and asked, "Please do not say anything to Adam until he has been here."

"Of course not, Chief Superintendent Young. I understand. Thank you for letting me know."

Mark faxed Adam.

Stan and Luke were at the station waiting for Adam on Saturday morning. The three of them walked and talked.

Amanda and Joan were praying for them.

Adam cried when he heard about the divorce, but he realised it was best in the circumstances for his dad to have some peace and a new start. He didn't want his dad to be hurt again. His mum was at that time still living with David, her new partner. He shared these thoughts with his dad, Mark and Luke, and they were very relieved at his mature way of reasoning.

Mark had previously discussed the situation with Amanda, Stan and Luke. They had realised Adam would be upset, and they wondered how they could console him. They thought of several things, but decided to ask him if he would like to go for a run in Stan's renovated 1970s Triumph Stag, which had passed all the tests.

When Mark suggested this to Adam, he was delighted.

Amanda asked, "Would you like to invite Robert to come to lunch and then go for a run with you?"

"Thank you, Amanda, but I would like time with my dad and Luke this afternoon. I would also like to go to The Open Church Youth Club this evening, please. May Robert come to dinner and go with me?"

"Of course, if that is what you want, darling. We will have dinner at 6 p.m."

Later she had a short time alone with Adam.

"I am upset, Amanda. She is my mum, but she made the choice and didn't consider us. It's a shame, but that is life."

Amanda was very impressed with his maturity. After they had talked, she asked him, "Could you possibly have time to design our wedding invitations?"

He was delighted.

She had hesitated to ask him this, but earlier she had talked with Stan, Mark and Luke and they had advised her to play it by ear. Now she went for it, and she was very glad of his attitude.

She hugged him and told him, "You are a precious brother to me."

He laughed.

Mark rang Robert's dad, the Reverend Brian, to tell him about this latest happening, and he had asked for his prayers – likewise with Matthew, his vicar at The Open Church.

Luke rang Matthew and told him, "I am bringing Adam and Robert to the youth group; I will stay with them and bring them back."

Matthew told him, "The youth leaders will welcome this. They have booked the swimming pool for games."

"That's brilliant, Matthew! Thank you. We will all be coming tomorrow morning."

Adam then rang Robert: "Would you like to go to The Open Church Youth Club with Luke and me this evening? They are going for swimming games."

"That will be brilliant, thanks, Adam."

"We will fetch you at about 5 in dad's 1970s Triumph Stag ready for 6 p.m. dinner."

Brian and Robert were eager to see this car on the road.

Amanda didn't invite anyone to come back with them for Sunday lunch. She wanted it to be a family occasion before Adam went back to Cambridge.

Stan, Mark and Luke took him back to the railway station. Whilst he was travelling he began designing the wedding invitations.

They dropped Luke at the fitness club, and then Stan went sketching by the river. Mark and Amanda had a swim and talk.

"I think your mum should be invited to our wedding, darling, but not David. We must ask your dad first, of course, in a few days' time."

"That's very generous of you, sweetheart; but if she accepts, who will escort her?"

"That's another thing to discuss with your dad."

"Will your parents approve?"

"Yes. They are very compassionate and wouldn't want to hurt you or spoil your day."

"Race you to the side," said Mark grinning.

She knew he wanted to kiss her.

When Adam came the following weekend, they discussed this invitation with him and he expressed a wish to escort his mum.

Chapter 11

Amanda's parents, Joshua, Nicola and family, and Luca came up for the engagement party. Marcos had come the day before to help the Morley chefs. Bob, of course, was invited with Miss Biggin. It was a low-key party. The Contessa had had a ring Amanda had loved since she was a little girl cleaned up, and Luca had previously brought it. Mark agreed that if it was what Amanda wanted, so be it.

He had had made a bone-china full tea service with a sweet-pea design for Amanda's afternoon teas. She loved it.

Amanda bought him a mobile phone with all the latest technology. He was thrilled. It would be so useful to him in his work.

The next few weeks were hectic. Amanda had a new exercise regime as she was now able to swim for longer periods. Lady Teresa's secretary sent out all the invitations for the wedding, and the royal family promised to fly down from Balmoral.

Amanda's dress of white silk was made by Jean and other expert dressmakers from the WI. It was in a classic style, in keeping with Lady Amanda. The Contessa sent her the diamond tiara and necklace by way of Count Luca.

Joshua and Nicola's two daughters' bridesmaids' dresses were made in London. The girls were so excited. Their basket of flowers and Amanda's bouquet, including of course sweet peas, were to be arranged by the Brookwell WI flower arrangers. A giant marquee was erected in Amanda's parents' grounds.

Mark asked Brian if he would sing, during the service, 'May the Lord Bless You and Keep You' and he suggested that the choir could join in near the end while he and Amanda sat quietly.

Brian was overwhelmed at being asked. He and his family, Hugh and his family and Jean, the dressmaker, were invited to Lord and Lady Dansie's for lunch before the wedding rehearsal. Their transport would carry the wedding dress and veil as well as flower arrangements, which were kept in a cold store. Robert and Matthew were to be part of the sidesmen's team. They were all booked into the hotel that was hosting Mark's stag night.

An expert organic gardener asked Amanda and Mark if he could have the job of head gardener (he was very friendly with Mrs Burton). After a short interview, they welcomed him.

Mark and Luke emptied a big concrete trough, and filled it with soil and 'special' compost. Mark fetched pots of sweet peas and gypsophila from the local nursery; he decided to sow seeds in the autumn.

Lord and Lady Hayward hadn't had a kitchen garden, but a gardener grew flowers for the house and kept the yards clean. He asked to stay on. They drew up plans for the garden and the local builders built a wall of open blocks to let light and air through but keep the animals out. They brought in a digger and a plough to dig up the area; they made paths, laid a foundation and built a wall three metres high for a large greenhouse with self-opening windows. A watering system using the spring water was installed, and heating wires were laid.

Mark asked permission to have wind turbines set up at the top of their field. He also asked Amanda if he might have a small greenhouse to grow sweet peas, freesias, chrysanthemums, etc. for her; also, when their children were growing up, he hoped they would have an interest in watching plants grow. The 'special' compost was spread over the entire garden. A chicken run was built. The copse beside the gypsy camp was fenced off as promised, and all the traps were moved from the wood. The Shulots' dogs still had the run of the grounds during the night, and all the Chiverton dogs were great friends with them.

As Mark was crouching down feeling the texture of the soil, he caught Amanda looking at him. He stood up, wiped his hands on his handkerchief and said, "Lady Amanda and I need a few minutes alone." He wheeled her chair down to the seat under the umbrella and sat down. He gently said, "I spotted you looking at me, sweetheart."

She blushed. "Yes."

"Have you ever seen a nude man?"

"Not in the flesh."

Mark asked her, "When Andrew held you close, did you feel him?"

"Yes, a few times, but he quickly moved away."

A pang went through Mark. "Right, darling, though I long to hold you close I discipline myself. Do you understand, Amanda?"

"Yes. I know the birds and the bees!"

Mark laughed, squeezing her shoulder.

Amanda asked him, "Am I being unfair?"

"No, you are not. I am very proud of you. I still cannot believe you are going to marry me – I have to keep pinching myself. But please don't be shy about asking me anything you are doubtful about.

Amanda assured him she would. She told him he would make her a wonderful husband, physically and mentally, and that he would be a marvellous daddy to their children. "I long to be in your arms. I adore you," she told him.

They kissed.

Amanda asked, "May I ask you something, Mark?"

"Of course, darling. Ask anything."

"Have you had any relationships?"

"Yes, precious, I have had one."

Jealousy tore through her.

"It was several years ago – we were both at a low ebb. It was nothing, darling. She is now enjoying her career in London."

She then asked, "Are you still in touch?"

"No, it was just a weekend. Please forget it, sweetheart. If I could now undo it, I would."

They kissed again.

"We had better go back and sort this garden out. I can see I will need plenty of organic food if I am to help you produce our children," he teased her.

Amanda laughed. "We had better get on with growing them, then."

Amanda was filled with a confident maturity. She and Mark had a new closeness, and everyone noticed it.

Amanda later told Joan, "I am now so relaxed with Mark. He has told me to discuss anything with him."

Joan was so thankful. "This is a vital part of your relationship, now and after you are married. Good girl, darling! I am so proud of you. Mark is a wonderful man – I am so proud to know him."

Amanda replied, "So am I."

Mark had begun supporting a local charity which helped men who had been injured in Afghanistan. He was told of a local man who had lost an arm, and his face and neck were badly scarred; he suffered bad nerves and couldn't work. Mark asked Amanda if she thought he could be given the job of caretaker/gatekeeper. The dogs would be running free and he could make sure there was no danger of them attacking anyone. Albert was married and had two little boys, but life hadn't been good for any of them since his injury. His boys had been causing problems at school. Mark suggested they buy a caravan for his daytime use.

Amanda said, "We had better discuss this with him."

Albert came. They were very impressed and the dogs accepted him.

Amanda asked if he could arrive for 7 a.m., ready for the milkman and post. Steven, one the gardeners, would collect these for the house. His working day, Monday to Saturday, would finish at 12.30 p.m.

Albert said, "Yes, I accept, ma'am, sir. Everything will be safe with me, and I thank you from the bottom of my heart for this opportunity."

Amanda asked, "How will you get here?"

"I will walk, ma'am. I live not far away – actually in one of your houses."

"Right," said Amanda, "we will buy you a caravan with a television, etc. If there is anything else you will need, please let Chief Superintendent Young or myself know."

Mark had a security camera put on the caravan and a telephone so Albert could ring the house if unexpected visitors came requesting entrance. This was a new beginning for Albert and his family.

In the afternoons a disabled lady who knitted for charities did the job.

Chapter 12

Ten days before Amanda was due to return to hospital for her second X-ray, Sir Philip rang her. He had had a breakthrough. Mr Hughes, the eminent American surgeon, with the help of technicians, had made a plastic elbow and inserted it successfully into a shattered elbow. Mr Hughes told Sir Philip that they had almost perfected a plastic knee; this was a more difficult operation, but they said they would love to help Lady Amanda if possible. A few days later Mr Hughes rang Sir Philip to tell him they had the knee ready, and they arranged to visit Amanda with a technician. The Commander agreed to be a guinea pig for others who could not have a straightforward knee operation. In return, the operation would be free. Sir Philip invited Mr Hughes and an assistant to stay with him and his wife, and he asked Amanda to come to the hospital.

"This is good news, ma'am. Keep praying! If your bones and tissues have healed sufficiently, and there is no infection, the operation will go ahead. You will be given the greatest care."

Amanda texted Mark, and his senior gave him a few days' leave. Mark then rang Reverend Brian, who set a prayer-chain going.

Mr Hughes and Sir Philip held a press conference explaining the operation. Lady Amanda would be the first to undergo the new treatment. They showed a model of the knee.

Later, Sir Philip gave another press conference to say it had been a satisfactory operation. He announced that Lady Amanda was healthy and fit, the tissues and muscles had healed; the plastic knee had been inserted into the joint. "It has been very tricky, and Lady Amanda has to lie still for two days before beginning gentle, short exercises. She will stay in the hospital for at least six days and then she will be carefully taken on a stretcher back to Chiverton. She will have to wear a support for three months, but after six weeks, when the plastic has set, she will be able to bend her knee. At this stage we do not know how far. We have an exercise programme for her to follow. For at least a year Lady Amanda will return to hospital every three months for X-rays. Mr Hughes will keep in touch with me, as we monitor her progress. We regret Lady Amanda will still be using her support sticks when she marries Chief Superintendent Young in September. Also, regretfully, Lady Amanda will be unable to ride her horse, Tarquin, or any horse. In time she will only need one support.

After the two days, Mark returned to work. He obviously didn't want to leave Amanda, but he had to set a good example to his colleagues – no way would he ask for preferential treatment. Amanda admired him for this. Joan was with her.

It was the day before the wedding. Amanda, Mark, Joan, Luke, Adam, Stan and Bob were taken in Luca's plane from a local airfield to Elmwood. The men's suits were safely protected.

Luke set the camera ready to film the service inside the church, and a colleague operated it. Dougie's cameramen were also discreetly filming outside. They had promised to let the BBC (Derbyshire and Yorkshire networks) have a copy of the film. The press were not allowed inside.

After lunch they all set off to the beautiful old church. Chosen singers made up the choir, and Amanda and Mark had spent a long time on the music and hymns. The church was magnificent – full of flower arrangements. The perfume was outstanding – the sweet peas would be put in the next day. The musicians began the rehearsal, and Amanda walked proudly down the long aisle on her support sticks, with her dada holding her elbow.

When they reached Mark, he and Amanda burst out crying – the music was so emotional.

Joshua's three-year-old, Susan, asked in a loud voice, "Why are they crying, Daddy? Don't they want to get married?"

This caused an uproar.

The rehearsal promised a beautiful service.

They all went back to Elmwood, and Amanda rested her leg.

After dinner she and Mark had a short walk in the wood. Then he and the men went to the hotel for the stag party.

Early the next morning, Mark rang Amanda: "No, no one had been drunk – you can be proud of us." He said, "See you later, sweetheart. Don't be late, please."

She promised: "I will not. I adore you."

He told her, "I adore you too. I still cannot believe you are marrying me."

Lady Teresa's hairdresser and assistant came, and a beautician arrived to give them their make-up. When the bridesmaids were ready, they looked wonderful with their baskets of flowers. The maid and Jean dressed Amanda and fitted the tiara and veil. Her sticks had a trailing bouquet of sweet peas attached; she looked absolutely radiant and regal. Her mother started to cry.

Amanda laughed. "You will ruin your make-up!"

Her dada came into the downstairs room, and when he saw her he just stood and said, "You have always been beautiful, but today you are even more so. I loved you before you were born and have always loved you. I am so proud of you. Now, darling, you have been my little girl, but today you are going to be Mark's wife. It is the beginning of your new life. I couldn't be more pleased, and I wish you and him every happiness."

Amanda told him, "I have always loved you and appreciated you."

He said, "Time to go! We mustn't keep Mark waiting."

They went out to cries of "Oo, how beautiful!"

Jean and Sandra helped her into her car, and then raced to the car in front to get to the church in time to help her out. This went smoothly. The press and television crews were waiting, and they all called out, "Good luck, ma'am" and "Well done, ma'am."

Luke heard them and told Mark, "Amanda is here." He then told Mark, "Stay with me; she will come to you."

Mark was crying, so Luke gave him a handkerchief.

Everyone laughed.

Amanda came up the aisle. Although she was on her sticks, she appeared to glide. Her dada was lightly holding her elbow. Everybody gasped at her beauty – she looked very regal. She had eyes for no one but Mark.

When she reached him he told her, "You look absolutely glorious – you have glided up."

She said, "You have scrubbed up well!"

They all laughed.

Her leg support was in place in front of a padded chair. Mark helped her to the chair, and he sat with her. They stood in all seriousness and reverence to make their wedding vows.

There were some whistles when she promised Mark to obey him. The music, the Bible readings, the Bishop's words, Reverend Brian and the choir singing 'May the Lord Bless You and Keep You', Mark singing 'At Last' whilst they were signing the register: everything about the service was so holy.

When she and Mark walked down the aisle as man and wife, both radiant, everybody started clapping! They laughed. Amanda and Mark bowed to the Queen, who was clapping and had tears in her eyes. Then Amanda and Mark reached Luke's camera, and they smiled into it especially for the Contessa. As they left the church, everyone was still clapping and outside people were cheering.

They stood at the top of the steps. Mark had his arm around her, waiting for the Queen, Prince Philip and other members of the royal family. Princess Anne gave her a horseshoe. After Amanda's parents and everyone had come out and the photographers and films had finished, they set off to Elmwood.

The official photographs were taken. It was a perfect summer day. They all went in for a most marvellous meal and the wines were the very best. Commissioner Johnson sat next to the Queen, as he had in church at Amanda's request. He looked so happy, and the Queen was happy and relaxed too – they all were.

The Queen congratulated Mark on his singing of 'At Last'. "That was perfect whilst you were signing the register."

Amanda smiled. "I heard him, ma'am."

The Queen and Prince Philip said, "We are looking forward very much to your coming to Balmoral."

Mark and Amanda replied, "Thank you, ma'am, sir. We look forward to it too."

When Joshua gave his speech, he made it humorous. He warned Mark that when she no longer needed the sticks he had better watch out. "She likes throwing people about," he said.

They all laughed.

Then he put an L-plate around Amanda's neck (she was blushing) and one around Mark's (he was laughing). Joshua went on to say, "Amanda and husband [everyone cheered] won't be staying too long at the reception. They have some practising to do!"

Lady Teresa said, "Really, Joshua!"

Everybody clapped and cheered.

They all went out of the marquee into the grounds whilst the tables were cleared away – discreet security was tight for Her Majesty and family. They returned as tasteful music was played. Amanda on her supports and Mark began the dance. He had his arm around her.

They sat and everyone came and congratulated them and said what a wonderful wedding it was. The Commissioner danced with the Queen! Prince Philip danced with Lady Teresa. The Queen, Prince Philip and family left at 4 p.m. Amanda and Mark went to get changed, and at 6 p.m. the helicopter came for them, Joan, Sandra and Julian and took them back to Chiverton. Lord Dansie had ordered a coach to take Stan and family back to Chiverton, and all the other guests back home.

When Amanda and Mark arrived at Chiverton the dogs were so excited and chased round. The Morley chefs prepared a meal for nine o'clock.

It was still a beautiful hot day. Amanda in her chair, Mark and Joan went down to the river, and then sat outside.

Amanda rang her parents: "Thank you for the wonderful wedding you have given us."

Mark thanked them for "your wonderful daughter", and he said, "I still can't believe she has married me!"

He promised them again, "I will take the greatest care of her and keep her happy; thank you again for the marvellous day."

Amanda said, "Everyone has enjoyed it – we certainly have. I'll be in touch tomorrow."

Her dada said, "You enjoy your honeymoon – don't bother about us."

Amanda laughed.

After greeting the gang, Luke said, "I have given the Queen's bodyguard a copy of the wedding film, also Count Luca's pilot a copy for the Contessa."

Amanda and Mark both said, "Thank you. We are very grateful."

He said, "I greatly enjoyed doing it – it makes a change from the fitness! Adam and I will get on transferring more copies."

They thanked him and Adam again, said "night-night" and went up to their rooms. They spoke with the Contessa, telling her, "It has been a wonderful day. Luca is bringing you a copy of the film. We love you and are so grateful to you."

She rebuked them, saying, "It is I who am grateful to you for bringing me so much happiness and peace. I know Amanda is safe with you, Mark." She jokingly said, "Go on, you two, you have better things to do than talk to me on your wedding night!"

Sandra knocked on the door. "Your meal is here, ma'am, sir."

She and Julian had brought it up in the lift.

They thanked her, and, when they had gone, Mark wheeled the trolley in. The dogs were downstairs with Stan and Joan, and they enjoyed their first private meal as man and wife.

Next morning they had arranged for breakfast to be served at 9 a.m. When they went down, Bob had already arrived. Everyone was happy and relaxed. Amanda thought she would be shy, but she wasn't – they were her family. They all had a good breakfast. Mrs Burton, Sandra and Julian came in; then, over coffee, they began to watch the film.

Amanda and Mark sat on the settee with their arms round each other for the first time in front of other people. They were all thrilled with the film and congratulated Luke and Adam. It was marvellous to see Mark and Luke arriving, and then the royal family and everyone else.

When Amanda arrived at the church they were all thrilled to see how she got out of the car and set off down the aisle. She looked radiant, and her dada was bursting with pride. It was wonderful to have a record of that day. They all went to look at the wedding presents; Mark suggested they put a thank you in the papers for the time being. They agreed this was a good idea.

Later they were going to have a large marquee put up and hire portable loos, and they decided to invite on three or four Saturday afternoons the local police for sandwiches, cakes, beer, etc. In this way, shift workers wouldn't miss out.

Chapter 13

On Sunday morning, Luke and Stan took Amanda, Mark and Joan to the airfield nearby, where Luca and one of his private planes was waiting. He kissed Amanda's hand, and greeted Mark and Joan. The bodyguard said good morning. They boarded and took off. Luca had very experienced pilots.

They were served with a glass of wine each and Luca prepared them: "As you know, the Contessa isn't well. I have to tell you, she didn't want the doctor to contact you before your wedding, but you must know now that your aunt has at the most two or three weeks to live."

Amanda, horrified, cried, "Oh no! Please, God, not that!"

"Yes," said Luca, "she has kept up her strength for your wedding and your arrival today."

Amanda looked at Mark and asked, "Is there any possibility we can take her home to Chiverton?"

Luca was adamant. "Sorry, no. Please do not let her see you upset. You are all trained and intelligent, but it will be hard."

They promised.

"Of course," Amanda told him, "we appreciate you telling us so we are prepared."

He said, "The specialist will see you."

When they arrived at the villa, they hurried to see the Contessa. They were all shocked to see how fragile she was, even though they had seen her on the computer camera link many times.

They had lunch together and they all spoke in Italian. Then, whilst the Contessa and Joan went for a rest, Amanda and Mark went up to the lake and cave. Mark was overwhelmed. They gathered wood for a fire in the cave. They made love in the cave then swam, lit the fire and made love again.

Amanda said, "Although the shadow of the news of my aunt is hanging over me, I have never known such happiness; I have realised how lonely I have been."

He held her close and admitted, "I too have been very lonely."

Mark then told her, "When speaking with your aunt using the computer camera link, she told me that all she wanted was for her beloved Amanda to be happy. You have made her life happy and full of joy." Mark said, "I promised her that, whatever happened, I will look after you and make you happy and secure.

After dinner, Amanda played the piano and she and Mark sang.

The Contessa told them and Joan, "You mustn't be sad. I have had a fulfilled life and Amanda has been my greatest joy. I should have listened to her years ago when she asked me not to smoke – but there we are, we all make mistakes."

They agreed.

Mark told her and Joan, "You must stay here; I have to return to work. I will ask for compassionate leave to be with you when the time comes."

Everyone respected him for not taking advantage of his position.

When the Contessa had gone to bed, the specialist arrived and, after seeing the Contessa, he spoke with them: "I regret we are now looking at hours, not days."

Amanda cried, "Oh no!"

He told them, "The Contessa is now ready to be rid of her sufferings, but she doesn't know how soon the end will be. I thank God you are able to be here."

Amanda was heartbroken. She said, "My mum ought to be here."

The specialist advised her, "Wait another day. The Contessa wants to be with you and Mark as much as possible."

Next morning Sophie said, "I would love Mark to have some Italian shoes and suits."

To please her, whilst she was being attended to they went to the shoe shop. The assistant told Mark, "We will deliver tomorrow to the villa, sir. Now we have your last, just ring us and we will send to England."

Mark had never had such comfortable shoes – he ordered two more pairs.

Joan bought some very special three-ply wool to use on her new knitting machine. She hadn't been able to obtain any locally or in London. She also bought hanks of silk to knit with. The assistants promised to post supplies to her in England when necessary. The Contessa's companion offered Amanda and Joan rolls of beautiful coloured silk and Italian lace, which they could have made up by Jean. They were all trying to act normally.

Although the specialist had said not to send for Lady Teresa, Amanda, after asking Joan and Mark's advice, had rung her with the specialist's prognosis. Luca fetched her.

Joan woke Amanda, Mark and Lady Teresa in the early hours. "Come urgently," she said. "The Contessa is at the end."

The priest arrived.

Amanda begged the Contessa, "Please do not leave me."

She said, "You have Mark now. Please have lots of babies."

Mark promised. "We will, I pray, Contessa."

She thanked Amanda for all the happiness she had given her and then breathed her last.

Mark rang Amanda's dada, Joshua, Chiverton and his senior officer.

After breakfast, the solicitor took Mark to buy a suit, shirt and tie for the funeral. The jacket had to be altered, but they delivered the next day. Amanda sent a personal shopper for suitable clothes, etc. for her, her mum and Joan. Everyone was upset at the Contessa's death. It was broadcast on TV and radio, and the newspapers were full of it.

Gessi, the solicitor, let Dougie and the BBC know of the Contessa's death. The cremation was fixed for that Thursday. Amanda's family came to be with Amanda and pay their respects.

The solicitor, Amanda, Lady Teresa and Luca, with the Contessa's companion, prepared the service and decided whom to invite. Amanda invited Dougie to come with the manager of the Contessa's London store, and Mr and Mrs Goodall, the owners of the glass factory. She arranged with Luca to have them fetched.

Dougie asked, "May my cameraman film?"

Amanda answered, "You can film the arrival at the

crematorium. I have asked the press not to take photographs inside."

Amanda and Mark led the procession behind the coffin. It was a beautiful service with a filmed tribute to the Contessa.

During lunch, Amanda asked the Contessa's friends and colleagues if they could let Gessi have any tributes and photographs for an Italian TV programme. They were all honoured at being asked, and promised to get on with this immediately. The Contessa had been such a wonderful lady. They all raised their glasses to her memory.

After lunch, many of the Contessa's friends and colleagues left; the ones the solicitor had invited to stay for the reading of the will joined Amanda and Mark.

Amanda was the main benefactor, as they knew: the villa, all the contents, the one-third share in the London store, the other property and shares, and the undisclosed money were hers. The Contessa's companion, doctor, nurses, housekeeper, staff and Miss Joan all received a generous money legacy.

Luca's pilots took them all back home. Luca had made Amanda promise to let him know when she wanted to return to the villa or travel anywhere. Jack, the British solicitor, had to stay a further couple of days with Gessi to help sort out transferring everything into Amanda's name.

Dougie, in his programme, showed the arrival of the funeral cars and said, "The Contessa has been part owner of Mason's, the London store, which sold British goods here and abroad, providing employment for hundreds of people. She also supported the Bryden glassware factory. The Contessa rescued the Bryden factory when it was closing due to lack of orders. This was a great blessing to the area and boosted the local economy; she introduced the glassware to Italian stores. All the British and Italian charities she supported were greatly blessed. The Contessa admitted she should not have smoked – she ought to have listened to her beloved Amanda years ago; although very ill she had hung on until she saw Amanda married to Chief Superintendent Young. They and Lady Teresa were with her when she died. It was a terrible shock when the specialist warned them that the Contessa would only last two or three days when

Lady Amanda and Chief Superintendent Young went to spend their honeymoon with her. Lady Amanda is heartbroken. She had expected her adored aunt to live to see their first baby at least. They hadn't been told previously just how ill she was. She didn't want to spoil the wedding or have them cancel, she was so happy that with the specialist's help she had managed to keep mobile."

Luca took them all back. He made Amanda promise to let him know when she wanted to return to the villa or anywhere.

Amanda thanked him and said she hoped to see him at Chiverton shortly.

He accepted with delight.

Amanda, her mum and the Italian solicitor, Gessi, had put a tribute in the local Italian papers.

Amanda and Mark invited the Italian media to Chiverton to make a documentary of the Contessa's life. They agreed and, on receiving the tributes from Gessi, sent them with questions and suggestions for approval.

Luca said to Amanda, "I will pick up everything from Gessi, then collect your mum and bring her to Chiverton to co-ordinate with you and me what Jake will need."

After they had sorted out the film clips and photographs, he took Lady Teresa back home – they didn't want to spoil Amanda and Mark's time together.

Jake and the crew arrived at the Morley and, after breakfasting there, they came to Chiverton to set up. Luca brought Lady Teresa back. The crew filmed a dummy run.

Lady Teresa opened the documentary and then Amanda continued. The crew, as in London, had their lunch whilst putting the photographs and video clips in.

After lunch they watched the film, and made a few additions and alterations. It was all in Italian, filmed with clever techniques. Subtitles in English were added later.

Everyone was delighted with the finished product. It was worthy of the Contessa. It would be broadcast in Italy on the following Saturday evening. The crew gave Amanda two copies, loaded their gear and returned to Italy. Lady Teresa and Luca went back to London with a copy. To relax, she and Mark went for a swim.

Bob and Jack, the local solicitor, came to dinner and then they all watched the film.

Stan, Bob and Luke all agreed: "We would love to have known her."

They all congratulated Amanda for her setting this documentary up.

Jack said to Amanda, "I will need to see you in a few days, ma'am."

"Of course."

Jack took Mr and Mrs Goodall a video of the film.

The programme was received with rapture everywhere – everyone was as proud of it as they had been of the Contessa.

The following Friday in the early evening, Amanda, Mark, Joan, Stan and Bob went to the villa in one of Luca's planes. Mrs Burton put fresh steaks and chicken, etc. in a frozen-food container. Luke stayed at Chiverton to attend to the dogs, and he and Adam arranged to go later.

Stan and Bob were overwhelmed by the villa, the lake and the cave. They said, "We will make sure you both have privacy – after all, you are still on your honeymoon!"

They both said they were looking forward to buying more Italian shoes. Joan was looking forward to buying more wool, etc.

Amanda was embarrassed at having to speak in Italian, as Stan and Bob did not know the language. They said they were thoroughly enjoying themselves. They were so pleased to be there.

The next morning the Italian solicitor came to see Amanda, and Mark, Joan, Stan and Bob went for a walk.

The housekeeper, Miss Louis, and staff congratulated Amanda on the tribute to the Contessa.

Amanda asked them, "Will you stay on? My family and friends will be coming for holidays."

They were delighted.

Amanda said, "Chief Superintendent Mark and I will be coming some weekends, but I pray we will be starting our family soon."

Miss Louis asked Amanda, "Have you any long-term plans for the villa, ma'am?"

Amanda answered, "We are carefully thinking. Would you be happy if it became a holiday home to accommodate family, friends, and honeymoon couples later on? There is no immediate rush."

She replied, "Oh yes, ma'am. There is a great demand for accommodation – for people coming to the operas. We have been afraid you will sell."

Next morning, Miss Louis asked Amanda to excuse her. "May I have a word with you and Chief Superintendent Young when convenient?"

Amanda looked at Mark and asked, "What about? We will be free after breakfast."

Miss Louis said, "Thank you, ma'am."

Joan, Stan and Bob prepared to have a local walk. Amanda and Mark conversed to the staff in Italian.

Miss Louis said, "The chef has asked me to speak to you, ma'am, sir. As both of you enjoy Italian food, he wondered if you had a vacancy for him at Chiverton?"

Amanda was surprised. She asked, "Isn't he happy here?"

"Yes, ma'am. He adored the Contessa, and the Contessa greatly respected him and was very fond of him; but now your aunt isn't with us and his parents are getting elderly, he would like to be nearer them. They adopted him when they were in their forties, and they were wonderful parents. He thought this would be an opportunity. I have to tell you, ma'am, sir, that Gerald is British."

"I am surprised. He speaks and looks Italian."

"He comes from Brookwell!"

Amanda asked, "Brookwell near us?"

"Yes, ma'am. He came here four years ago to improve his Italian when he finished university. He loves cooking Italian food." She continued: "He specialised in cordon bleu cookery, preparing, etc. at university. He is fanatical about cleanliness and his manners are perfect. All of us and the local people would be sad to see him leave, but we understand his commitment to his parents."

Amanda said, "We have been borrowing chefs from the Morley, but it is getting awkward for them as they are so busy at this time of year. We had better discuss it with him.

"Yes, ma'am. Would you and sir like a drink?"

"Yes, please – coffee."

Gerald came in. He said in English, "Good morning, ma'am, sir."

Amanda asked him, "Would you like to converse in Italian?"

He replied, "Thank you, ma'am."

The waitress brought the coffee in and, when they were served, Amanda said, "Miss Louis has put us in the picture about your parents. She tells us you are interested in coming to Chiverton to be our chef?"

"Yes, ma'am, sir."

Amanda told him, "I and the Chief Superintendent adore Italian food, but some of the relatives who live with us prefer British food."

Gerald said, "That will be no problem, ma'am. I can prepare and cook all kinds of foods. The Contessa preferred plain food for the last two years. She ordered Italian food when you came here, ma'am, because she knew you preferred it."

Amanda said, "I didn't know that."

Mark said, "You will appreciate that we will need police and health checks."

"Of course, sir. I anticipated this and have already received them. I have my school and university references." He then passed an envelope to Amanda and Mark. "The local priest knows me well. I am a Roman Catholic. If I may add, ma'am, sir" – they nodded – "Miss Louis has informed you I was adopted" – they nodded again. "On my birth certificate it shows my real parents' names. My father is Italian and my mother is British."

Amanda and Mark listened intently.

"My father was eighteen years old and my mother was sixteen. My father's family wouldn't accept my mother as she wasn't born into a high social class and they thought she was below their standards. That is why I am adopted. My real mother has made a wonderful career in politics in London."

Amanda knew her.

"My father is Luis – – – – – – – – – "

Amanda also knew that side of his family.

"My father paid for me to go to university and he introduced me to the Contessa to be her chef."

Amanda said, "We thank you for telling us this, Gerald."

He then said, "You will appreciate, ma'am, sir, that no one knows this, but it is on my birth certificate."

Amanda asked, "Will you live with your parents?"

He said, "I would prefer to rent a small cottage or flat locally. My parents are active but they miss me now they are older." He added, "I went to school with the Morley chefs."

"Very good, Gerald. We will read the checks and references and see you later."

They met up again with Gerald in the afternoon, and told him, "We are delighted."

They already knew he liked dogs – they had seen him with the dogs living at the villa.

Amanda said, "We have a small self-contained flat near the kitchens at Chiverton if you are interested."

He said, "That will be useful for me to be on hand."

Amanda said, "We couldn't allow a live-in girlfriend."

"No, ma'am."

Amanda went on, "You will have to be in before 11 p.m unless it is an exception."

He replied, "I will honour that, ma'am. I like to keep a diary of the meals served, and I note those which are the most popular. I also prepare menus using local provisions when possible. These of course I will present for your approval, Lady Amanda."

Mark asked, "Have you any hobbies?"

He said, "I work out at a gym, run and cycle. I hope to meet up with my school friends to share these activities, sir."

Amanda and Mark said, "Good!"

Amanda said, "There is one more thing, Gerald: with respect to Mrs Burton and the other staff, will you keep your music or whatever quiet?"

He replied, "I am so glad you mentioned that. I wouldn't knowingly do anything to upset you and rock the boat."

They laughed.

"Right, Gerald," said Amanda, "ask Miss Louis when you can be released and then we will arrange for you to come." She asked, "Is there anything we can take back for you?"

He said, "There is my bicycle and my chef's knives."

"No problem," said Amanda.

His father later told him how privileged he was to be on Amanda's staff.

Amanda rang to inform Mrs Burton, and she was delighted that Gerald would be joining them.

"I remember him growing up – he was sports mad and loved cooking from a young age. He was no trouble to his parents. Everyone knew he had been adopted and thought he had Italian blood in him. Have I to start getting his flat ready, ma'am?"

"Yes, please."

Amanda rang her mum also, and she was delighted.

Amanda asked Gessi, "What do you think about the villa being used as a holiday home for a few people and honeymoon couples?"

He said, "That is an excellent idea – they would bring trade to the local area. Everyone is thinking, ma'am, that you will sell it now you are married and have your home in Derbyshire."

Amanda said, "No, but my husband and I will not be using it much after we have started our family."

Gessi said, "Ah, you will have beautiful bambinos."

They laughed.

Amanda went on, "Our family and friends will be coming for holidays too."

He said, "Good, good." He suggested, "You will need a manager, ma'am; and also, you could perhaps advertise the villa in exclusive magazines here and in America."

Amanda asked, "Will we be treading on anyone's toes?"

"No, no. There is a great need for accommodation, especially for the operas." (This was what the housekeeper had said.)

"Do you, ma'am, and the Chief Superintendent want me to oversee all this?"

Amanda was relieved. She said, "We shall be grateful."

She knew she could trust him. He knew about the Contessa's charities, so Amanda asked, "How much did she contribute?"

He told her that she helped the local hospital, and was especially generous in helping sick children and opera singers that had fallen on hard times.

Amanda asked, "Are the opera singers drug takers?"

He replied, "No, no, ma'am."

"Right, we will continue the giving. May I leave this with you also, Gessi?"

"Of course, ma'am. I want to do everything I can to help. I will inform them – they will be so grateful."

This good news was broadcast on TV and radio news and in the local newspapers. (Amanda received grateful thanks from everyone concerned.) Also, the good news was announced that Lady Amanda wouldn't be selling the villa but would later reveal

116

plans that would benefit the local shops. In the meantime, they said, her family and friends would be having holidays here. Lady Amanda and Chief Superintendent Young were going to start their family soon!

Gessi left. Amanda and Mark went to the cave and the lake. Naples, the Alsatian, went with them. The housekeeper was instructed to prevent anyone intruding on their privacy.

Later, when they saw the news and the papers announcing that they would be starting their family soon, Bob said, "They are as forthright as Derbyshire people!"

They all laughed and agreed.

Joan said, "They will all be buying baby wool!"

On Sunday, Count Luca took them to the local airfield, where Luke was waiting. He then went on to Amanda's parents for a meal before staying in London to deal with business matters.

Amanda rang him whilst he was still with her parents. "Thank you, Luca, for everything. You made it possible for me to travel and be with my aunt when she died."

He said, "The tribute to your aunt has been received with rapture in Italy. I am so grateful; people will be able to view their videos time and time again. I have never known anything so sensitive and beautiful and so quickly put together. Everyone is so proud of you, Amanda."

Amanda said, "Thank you again. We all are so grateful to you."

He said, "Anywhere you want to go, just let me know, darling. My pilots are at your command."

When Gerald arrived at Chiverton he brought from his Italian father, in appreciation of Amanda giving him this opportunity, a beautifully designed wooden box that contained a very excellent light flowery perfume – very exclusive – and beauty treatments.

Amanda asked Gerald to thank his father; she told him she would use the cosmetics with pleasure.

Chapter 14

Dougie rang saying, "We have the clips from the wedding film and the Contessa's funeral ready for your and Chief Superintendent Mark's approval."

Amanda asked, "Shall we say Thursday following your holiday with you all coming up on the Wednesday?" (Dougie and his family hadn't had a holiday for three years due to his television commitments.)

Amanda and Mark offered them the villa for a few days. They accepted with delight. Amanda arranged for them to visit Jake at his television studio.

"Let's go for that. My PA will book the Morley if possible."

She invited Dougie to lunch with them on Thursday.

"Thank you, ma'am."

"Dougie, I will fax the questions and suggestions as before. We will have photographs and video clips. Enjoy your holiday."

"Thank you, ma'am. You have no idea what this means to my family. I realise I have neglected them, but I will attempt to do better from now on."

"Good," laughed Amanda.

Amanda started on the questions and suggestions. She suggested photographs of Mark arriving at Ashwood and the dogs going potty with delight when they saw him; her, Mark and Joan planning a therapy programme with swimming twice a day; her exercising in her room in the evenings with Miss Biggin; her and Mark playing the pianos and singing; the quizzes; computer tennis; speaking to the Contessa on the computer camera link; Mark and Joan taking her down to the river in her chair with the dogs; Stan and Bob coming for lunch the next day; her with her new haircut; the Spring Fair; arriving at St James' on Sunday; Mark's promotion lunch and the musical afternoon; her interview with Dougie; and the remaining members of her team coming for the weekend.

Mark and Joan approved these suggestions.

Mark asked his superior for the Thursday morning off, and he gave him the day. Mark had worked through several lunch hours and had made up time at home on his laptop.

Dougie began by asking Mark, "Sir, when did you know you were in love with Lady Amanda?"

Mark answered, "From the moment I saw her – this beautiful vision. Then, as we were getting to know each other I picked up vibes that Lady Amanda was growing fond of me. I couldn't believe it. This gorgeous, beautiful lady – beautiful inside and out – super-intelligent, and the top police lady at the Met was actually beginning to like me and wanted to be in my company."

Amanda butted in: "I loved you," and they gazed into each other's eyes.

Dougie cleared his throat.

Mark went on, "I had to keep pinching myself that I was actually with her."

"When did you know, ma'am?"

"It was when Mark first arrived. My dogs are trained to be wary of strangers."

"I know that well, ma'am. [Here a photo was shown of the dogs growling at Dougie in his first interview with Amanda.] As I got to know him I knew in my heart he was the one for me. He is the one I want to spend my life with." They kissed. "I will always keep him happy and loved. We both have known grief – Mark's colleagues, including my fiancé, Andrew, were killed; and members of my team were killed whilst with me. Mark has helped me greatly."

Mark said, "Lady Amanda helped me greatly too. We shall never recover from these incidents in which young professional lives were lost, but we have to move on. We now have a better understanding of others' sufferings."

Dougie asked, "One aspect of your job, sir, deals with emotions and needs?"

"Yes."

Amanda said, "I don't know how I would have coped with the Contessa's sudden death if Mark hadn't been supporting me."

Video clips were then shown of Chiverton; her resignation; her accompanying her dada as he played the violin; singing with Mark; the rock-and-roll time with the Commissioner singing along; her and Mark's engagement; Amanda going back into hospital; Tarquin and Thunder arriving at Chiverton; and preparing for their wedding. Wedding clips showed Mark and Luke, her mum and family, and the royal family arriving at the church; Amanda and her dada walking down the aisle to Mark. Reverend Brian and the choir singing 'May the Lord Bless You and Keep You'; Mark singing 'At Last' whilst they signed the register; Amanda and Mark walking up the aisle together, bowing to the Queen and stopping and bowing towards the camera which was relaying the wedding direct to the Contessa; and outside with the royal family and her family. Finally, film was shown of her setting off to Lord and Lady Dansie's for lunch, and a photo of Amanda, Mark and Joan going back to Chiverton in Luca's helicopter.

"Sir, your wedding?"

"It was absolutely glorious. When Lady Amanda was coming up the aisle to me in that wonderful white dress, I was thanking God she had saved herself. There can be no greater gift a bride can give her husband."

Amanda said, "I also was very thankful." She told Dougie, "With Mark being nearby at Ashwood and then Chiverton there were times when I thought I wouldn't be strong enough. At these times I thought of Andrew and prayed to God."

Mark said, "Yes, it had been hard for me also. I also prayed for strength and used all my self-control because I knew we would both have regretted weakening."

Amanda said, "I would go up to my room after dinner to work through my routine."

Mark said, "I did some work on my computer and then ran with Luke and friends with the dogs." (Photographs of these activities were shown.)

Dougie asked, "Lady Amanda promised in her wedding vows to obey you?"

"Yes," laughed Mark, "that was a surprise, but with her SAS training tricks I know when to draw the line."

Amanda added, "I have only tried to drown you once!" and she kissed him again.

"Do you both work out?"

"Yes," they answered.

Amanda said, "I do special exercises for my knee. I will always look after myself; and I will always try to keep Mark in love with me. I have the wonderful example of my mum and Nicola – they always look their best for their husbands. My mum and dada have been married thirty-four years [photo] and Nicola always puts my brother Joshua first [photo]."

Photos were then shown of Amanda, Mark and Joan going to Italy in Count Luca's plane; arriving at the villa; and Amanda and Mark following the Contessa's coffin. The tape of Pavarotti singing was played over the video of the Contessa asking everyone not to be sad as she had had a wonderful life. In this video the Contessa said she regretted not listening when her beloved Amanda asked her not to smoke, and she said she especially wanted Amanda and Mark to be happy at the beginning of their married life. She regretted she would not see their bambinos, but thanked Amanda for making her life so happy. She also thanked her sister, Lady Teresa, and Lord Jonathan, Joshua, Nicola, and their family. The sequence concluded with Pavarotti singing while Amanda played the accompaniment.

Dougie asked them, "What is happening to Villa Verona? Have you thought of selling it?"

"No," said Amanda, horrified. "It is a precious link with my aunt. We have given it much thought and sought advice. Chief Superintendent Mark and I hope to start a family soon and will not travel, so it is going to be a holiday home for our family and friends, and some chosen families who appreciate Italy. There is a great need for accommodation, especially for the operas. The local people will welcome the extra trade they will receive from it."

"Have you upheld the charities your aunt supported in Italy?"

"Yes, out of respect for her. These charities were very precious to her. Some of the money we get from holidaymakers will go towards these charities."

Dougie said, "We all appreciate, ma'am, how you must miss your aunt."

"I do."

She began to cry, and Mark put his arms round her. The dogs came up to her.

Dougie looked uneasy, remembering the last time she had cried whilst with him.

"Several times a day I think, 'I will tell the Contessa that when I ring her this evening,' and then I remember I cannot."

Mark broke in: "Lady Amanda needs time to grieve."

"Of course, sir. We understand."

He asked, "Are you keeping your brain occupied, ma'am?"

Mark and Amanda laughed.

"Yes," she replied, "as I am Mark's wife, and mistress of Chiverton, there is something new every day. Also I research and compile quizzes for ITV and BBC – this is a great challenge and keeps me on my toes. I am also completing a children's book I began in my teens, and my brother-in-law Adam is illustrating it [photo]. My other brother-in-law, Luke, is a fitness trainer at the local police stations [photo of Luke lifting weights]. He has set up ongoing exercises for me as my leg has grown stronger. I am so greatly blessed with Mark's family [photo]."

"They live at Chiverton?"

"Yes. I am happy to say, they are a great help to us, as is Chief Inspector Hawkins [photo of them all together]."

"Lady Amanda, when you gave in your resignation you were asked by the Met to continue working from home in an advisory role?"

"Yes, and I did until the two cases I had been working on were completed. Then I decided it involved too much commitment."

Mark nodded.

"You had also previously been offered promotion?"

"Yes. If I hadn't met Mark, that would have been my next step; but God in His wisdom brought him to me and he is now my life. Being in this community is very precious to both of us, and Mark's job is very important to both of us – policing is in my blood. Mark is able to talk to me and I can understand. I am getting to know more and more people and their needs."

"You are also still involved with your charity in East London?"

"Yes, I am. Later on I am hoping to play a role helping young people in this area – possibly as a magistrate."

"They would be very blessed to have the benefit of your gifts of perception and compassion."

"Thank you, Dougie, but I am no pushover."

They all laughed.

Dougie then asked Mark, "What is your charity, sir?"

Mark answered, "A scheme to provide shelter and care for animal rescue. I joined this scheme when I was in my teens after finding a dog which had been cruelly treated." He and Amanda sat with set faces. "We both adore dogs."

Dougie said, "Yes, I have noticed," and the camera panned across to where all the dogs were lying down. He thanked them both for the interview. He and all the others knew that Amanda and Mark now wanted to be left alone to come to terms with the shock of the Contessa's sudden death.

Mark said, "We thank you for all your understanding and expertise."

Amanda echoed his thanks, and told Dougie, "Mark, my family and I respect and admire you."

The show concluded with Mark singing and Amanda playing 'Here's to the Heroes'. A shot was shown of Dougie fussing the dogs!

After this interview was shown, Mark had a real surprise. A recording administrator contacted him to ask if he would make a CD singing 'At Last' and 'Here's to the Heroes'. Mark agreed on the understanding that all the money he made would go to help those injured and disabled in the Afghanistan War. Amanda was so proud of him and for him. She was asked to sing 'Be Thou My Vision' and 'You'll Never Walk Alone'. Reverend Brian sang 'May the Lord Bless You and Keep You'.

Mark suggested, after getting their permission, that Brookwell Choir could also sing hymns on the CD. This was accepted with pleasure. The CD was a great success and money poured in for their charities. By popular demand, the recording company made Mark's 'At Last' into a single. Everyone was so proud and pleased.

Amanda and Mark didn't socialise in the evenings. They preferred to spend the time together and ate dinners on their own. Every Sunday, however, they invited friends to lunch.

The local police and families were all grateful to be invited to Chiverton for the Saturday afternoons. Amanda and Mark mixed with everyone. Bob was in charge of the beer! Luke organised a tug of war for the men. The Open Church Youth Club organised games for the children. Mr Shulot's son provided three donkeys for rides. These were very popular. Brookwell Male Voice Choir sang. Mark and Amanda had borrowed chairs and tables from Ashwood Community Hall. They had portable loos set up! The WI provided the refreshments. They used disposable cups and plates. An ice-cream van was available.

Everybody thoroughly enjoyed it and asked when they might come again.

After their marriage, Lord Richard and Lady Sarah came from America to live in Ashwood. Lady Cynthia moved into a smaller home, where she was very happy. Amanda already knew Richard slightly and after meeting Sarah the two women grew to love each other like sisters. They spent time together walking the dogs two or three afternoons a week. Sarah was highly intelligent and helped Amanda with her quizzes. Joan and Amanda continued to swim in the mornings. Bob came to lunch every day he was free. Aunt Cynthia also came often, and then in the afternoon she sketched and painted alongside Stan.

Chapter 15

After three months Amanda returned to the hospital. Her knee joint had recovered 90% of its flexibility and she hoped, in time, by continuing her exercises and swimming, to recover full flexibility. Amanda, Mark, Lady Teresa and Joan stood on the steps outside the hospital with Sir Philip, who gave the reporters this latest good news. As Amanda walked down the steps, everyone clapped and cheered.

A few reporters called out, "Will you be starting your family now?"

Mark laughed. "We will."

Everyone cheered again and wished them good luck.

Three weeks later, Amanda started with morning sickness! The scan showed twins – Amanda and Mark didn't ask the sexes. She sailed through the pregnancy but was careful not to put too much stress on her knee, and was delivered of a beautiful boy, with the look of Mark, and a beautiful girl with red hair! Amanda cuddled them, telling them, "We love you and you are very welcome." Mark cried and kissed them. Chiverton was a very happy household.

Piaceri, the famous film director, contacted Amanda through her mum; he had come to London from abroad and it was recommended to him that he watch Dougie's video of Amanda and Mark's interview, Amanda's earlier interview, and the tribute to the Contessa. He asked Amanda and Mark's permission to make a film from these. He assured them that the film would be tasteful and it would set a good example. After speaking to Lord Justice Jonathan, and later seeing the script, they agreed; but they did not allow it to be filmed at Chiverton as they wanted to increase their family. Lord Richard and Lady Sarah agreed to Ashwood being used for some of the scenes. The money Amanda and Mark received was invested, with Richard's advice, for their children for when they were eighteen years old.

Richard, Sarah's family in America, and Lady Cynthia were very thankful that Amanda and Sarah were such good friends. They had had doubts whether she would settle in England. Sarah had Tarquin at Ashwood and rode him on every opportunity. She also ran a keep-fit class in the Community Hall. Mark and Richard were very compatible too.

Mark and Amanda bought Joan a knitting machine and overlocker; and whilst Amanda and Sarah were together, she went to the local college two afternoons per week with three friends from the WI to learn how to use it and knit Fair Isle garments. She drove there in the new car she had bought from the legacy left her by the Contessa. Amanda and Mark adored her and were glad she was enjoying some freedom. Joan and Stan grew very close. Joan had her waist-length hair cut short; it now waved around her face and she looked ten years younger.

A year later, when Amanda had finished breast feeding, due to sharp teeth, she was pregnant again. This time the scan showed a big baby and a smaller one. She was very well, but she was so big that for the last two months she had to rest in her chair for a lot of the time. Her doctor advised a Caesarean, but she asked to be given the opportunity to have a natural birth.

When the pains started, the private ambulance was waiting outside and her parents had come up to be with her – Lord Justice Jonathan, Mark and Luke had been big babies.

Amanda said, "I need the loo."

The nurse brought a bedpan, but she insisted on going to the bathroom. Mark and Joan were very anxious. They helped her back to the doctor and the delivery bed. When Gary examined her he realised she had begun to dilate – he could see the head coming.

The nurses got into action, and a beautiful boy came out without too much difficulty. Amanda had strong muscles through always keeping fit and healthy. Mark cried. Joan texted Amanda's parents while Amanda cuddled the little boy, telling him how much they loved him and that he was very welcome. She then said, "You are going to take some filling!" He was yelling! He weighed almost five kilos! Mark cuddled and kissed him.

"Now," said Gary, "let's have the other one."

It was a little girl with fair hair, and she weighed 3½ kilos. She was crying. Amanda repeated to her what she had said to the other babies. She and Mark were so pleased and they thanked God.

"Right," said Gary, "another push! Only six stitches! Well done, ma'am."

"Hang on," urged Amanda, "there is another baby coming."

"No, Lady Amanda, it is the afterbirth."

She said, "I am not silly – there is another baby."

He looked. Black curly hair was coming out. Mark fainted. It was a lovely small girl with the look of the Contessa Sophie and Lady Teresa. She had been hidden behind her brother and sister. She was 2½ kilos. Amanda was thrilled.

Her parents and everybody rushed up from downstairs while Joan brought Mark round.

He said, "Never again! This is it! Amanda has had enough."

She asked, "Might we discuss this in two years?"

Everybody laughed.

"Right," said Gary, "everyone out!"

They carried her into the bathroom and then stitched her.

Gary sent for Mark, who couldn't stop crying with relief and happiness. Amanda smilingly greeted him with, "Three babies, two breasts!" The boy was already feeding from her. The nurses asked her to express milk into bottles to freeze, explaining that the boy was so big that he would need feeding more often. The Italians went wild over the news of a 'little Contessa'.

After the birth Gary kept her in bed for five days with short walks to the bathroom. She thankfully had no damage to her womb and, as with the twins, she quickly regained her figure.

Amanda said to Mark, "Only two more to go, darling."

"Never! You have done enough."

"May we discuss this in two years, darling?"

All the children were healthy and intelligent.

Sophie was dainty but had a giant personality. One Sunday morning when she was only just turned two, the young day nanny told Amanda and Mark, "Ma'am, sir, I am having a problem with Sophie: she refuses to get dressed, She is only in her panties!"

They went to see her, and found her sat on the floor surrounded by her clothes.

She told them, "Horrible clothes! I want clothes like this," and showed them a picture from the book she was holding of a little girl in black velvet trousers and a white frilly blouse.

Amanda said, "What do you say when you ask for something?"

"Sorry," she said: "please."

Mark said, "Perhaps your brothers and sisters don't like their clothes either. Please get dressed – you will be cold in church in just your panties!"

Sophie laughed and held her arms up to him.

He lifted her up. "Now apologise to Crystal and then pick up all these clothes; after breakfast we will have a round-the-table talk."

Amanda and Mark knew she had Italian genes. The other children liked their clothes, and hadn't even thought about them. Jean, the dressmaker, made Sophie velvet trousers and frilly blouses and new clothes for her sisters and brothers.

Three years later Amanda was delivered of another healthy boy. He has black, curly hair. Amanda is healthy and her knee is stronger, but she and Mark have decided this is the last one. They are very thankful for their lovely family. All the children are treated the same. They all have different personalities and are respected. They are all loved but not spoilt. Mark and Amanda adore each other and are wonderful parents.